The Messiah In India

By Alan Fensin

Cassandra Press
San Rafael, Ca.

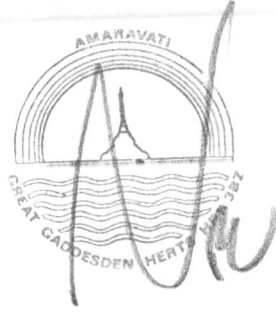

Cassandra Press
P.O. Box 868
San Rafael, Ca. 94915

Printed in the United States of America.

ISBN 0-945946-06-6

Library of Congress 89-62270

Front cover art designed by Susan St. Thomas.

TABLE OF CONTENTS

i i

Special thanks to Muslima Moonpaki for her editing and general collaboration on this novel.

INTRODUCTION

This novel is based upon ancient Tibetan documents first discovered by Nicolas Notovitch at the Himis monastery about twenty miles from the city of Leh located in the Himalayan mountains of Tibet just north of India. These documents were originally written on birch bark by the Brahmin priests of India almost two thousand years ago in the old Pali language. Notovitch had the document translated into Russian and brought this translation back to the west where it was then translated into English.

The existence of these ancient Tibetan documents was later confirmed by Swami Abhedananda and others who journeyed to the Himis monastery to verify the claims of Nicolas Notovitch. Swami Abhedananda later wrote a book titled *Kashmir O Tibbate* in which he gives a similar translation of the Tibetan document.

According to these ancient Tibetan documents, the Messiah did travel to various spiritual centers in India to perfect his spiritual realization. At the time, about two thousand years ago, India was at the center of the world's spiritual activity and would have been the natural place to get these teachings.

The ancient documents state that the Messiah spent twelve of his missing years in India, however this portion of the document is only a few pages long. The small amount of information covering the entire twelve years leaves much to the imagination. What could have happened during those twelve years? The Messiah would have certainly wanted to experience the spiritual life of India. India is a big country so he would have traveled far and wide throughout India, Tibet, and the Himalayas, from spiritual center to spiritual center and from teacher to teacher. Other teachings would have been obtained simply through occurrences during his travels, through clashes of culture and thought.

Surely there would have been one special teacher, a Master to provide special guidance. I have tried to bring this Master to life, realizing that he would himself be the sum of many teachings, many forms of mystical thought. Again, in India then as it still is now, there would have been many young disciples, many young seekers on similar paths to the Messiah. Let us imagine that the Master chose one to accompany him throughout his quest. Now we have two young men, one of whom is already marked by a very special destiny, under the protection of an immensely wise and kind old teacher, traveling through India as it must have been 2000 years ago.

In spite of the difference in time and space, some of the experiences encountered by the Messiah may hardly be any different from those of another person searching for spiritual enlightenment in this day and age. We each begin our temporal existence through a mystical conception when the spirit takes form as man. In this human form we attempt to solve the mundane conflicts we encounter; conflicts over survival, sexuality, and power. At some point, many of us find a way to accept ourselves and recognize and acknowledge our own divinity.

Alan Fensin

Chapter I

SURVIVAL

"I will meet him today," I thought as I awakened from a sleep full of dreams. My dreams had been of Essa, the man I was sent to meet. My spiritual teacher had told me a little about Essa, for Essa was no ordinary man, and I knew he would make a difference in my life. He was a member of a distant group of mystics called Essenes and, therefore, was called Essa.

I knew Essa would expand my awareness and influence my goal of spiritual illumination. He was already well known and admired throughout the northeastern section of India, for his healing powers as well as his wise teachings. It was said by some that the spirit of the infinite force was awake in this man.

The first bluish-white light of dawn shone over the crest of the distant hills. Beyond those hills and blending with the sky were the Himalayan mountains of northern India. I stood and stretched out the stiffness from my body. My campsite was surrounded by tall blue pines and located near a small rocky creek. I washed in its cold running water and rubbed myself dry and warm with my head cloth. I quickly dressed, filled a gourd full of water, and stuffed my blankets and few other belongings into my bundle.

My destination, the village of Sambalpur, was only a few hours away. In my haste and excitement, I skipped breakfast and departed for Sambalpur, eating a small bunch of bananas as I walked. In my anticipation of meeting Essa, I trampled steadily onward, without stopping to rest.

Sambalpur was a humble town, not unlike the many others scattered throughout this part of India. I walked quickly past the thatched roof and stick houses and headed to the public bazaar near the center of town where, I was told by the villagers, I would find Essa.

A large caravan had recently arrived at the caravansarai nearby on the plain. Now the marketplace was noisy and crowded with merchants and throngs of people milling about with every possible kind of foodstuff on their heads, in their arms, or displayed at their feet. The market, a covered structure, was packed with spices, grains, woven goods from mountainous regions, and cheap jewelry and spilled abundantly onto the neighboring alleys. Huge straw baskets and wooden bowls were filled to the brim with peanuts, rice, cashews, ginger roots, cardamon pods, spices, beans, chillies, loofahs, pineapples, limes, bread, fruits, roots, avocados, onions, garlic, gourds, tamarinds, ayurvedic potions and oils. Fresh vegetables and fruits were also stacked along the alleys where people elbowed each other, madly haggling over prices in several dialects.

Some areas of the market were reserved for basket weavers, jewelers, and incense and charcoal sellers. The tinkers, in dirty tattered rags and sackcloth, sat among heaps of rusty old items of every provenance, hammering away at tin cans and tin bowls. In a corner, dozens of chickens lay in a heap, their feet tied together and their eyes rolling wildly.

People were everywhere, scurrying around in turbans or saris, long colorful wool skirts, and embroidered goatskin vests. Sellers squatted in their stalls, eating chapattis and dahl from wooden bowls with their little children. Others squatted under someone else's stall and pulled at customer's pant legs or robe to point to their wares.

The entire market was a feast of bright colors, pungent smells, and constant din, each face a different color and shape, but always with the same intent look.

Still I looked for Essa whom I knew would stand out among the crowd. Pale and gentle-looking Essa. I lingered a moment near the stall of a spice and herb dealer, watched his children scurry under and around it, and delighted in the gaiety of their squeals. Then I continued my search for Essa.

I spotted a stall displaying colorful prayer wheels, prayer flags, religious wall hangings, amulets and talismans, a wonderful assortment of claws, tails, bones, teeth, crystals, and colored powders. I smiled at the proprietor and approached him. "Do you know where I might find a foreigner named Essa?

"No, I have never heard that name," he replied, brushing me away as if I were a nuisance.

I strolled to the other side of the bazaar and stopped at the stall of a fruit vendor. I stared hungrily at a basket of ripe mangoes. A young vendor with large gold bracelets around his arms noted my stare. He grinned and said, "Five mangoes for only two paise."

I handed him a five-paise coin as he gave me the mangoes, and I promptly ate one while I waited for my change. Instead of making change he began talking to another customer who had just entered the stall. "You still owe me my change," I demanded.

He looked at me with contempt and replied, "We're even. You gave me only five paise and that is the price.

"You said two paise!

"You're mistaken," he said and turned away to resume talking with his other customer.

I was dumbfounded and just stood there a few moments, disturbed that I had been taken advantage of. In a moment I would have shown this cheating merchant a lesson had I not looked beyond him at the new customer. He had long flowing hair that was parted in the middle, and he wore a full, but neatly groomed beard. He was dressed in a light linen robe and wool cloak.

"May I have a mango," the new customer asked?

"But of course," said the merchant and he handed him a mango. "It's a gift. There's no charge.

"Blessings be upon you for your generosity," replied the customer.

The irony of the situation did not escape me. This merchant was offering "generously" a mango for which I had already paid. I felt blinded with anger. My fists slowly clenched and unclenched themselves, and a wicked sentence was slowly shaping itself in my mind.

"Blessings to you, Essa," said the merchant.

Essa! I snapped out of my negativity and examined the customer. He was young, in his early twenties, yet exuded the maturity of a man much older than his physical age. He was tall, almost my height, and was obviously not an Indian. He appeared quite handsome, of proud bearing, yet nothing about him further distinguished him. Ah, yes! He was paler than most.

"Are you Essa?" I asked of him, realizing at once that this was an unnecessary question.

"Definitely," he responded. His voice was strong yet peaceful.

"I am Lamas and have been sent here by my teacher, Bentell," I quickly replied.

"I have been waiting for you," Essa beamed. His smile radiated warmth toward me. His eyes seemed to penetrate my soul. He had not the slightest trace of that insincere manner I often encountered in others, who rushed through their greetings, half-resenting the little time it took them.

Essa moved closer to me and placed his hand on my arm. "Please tell me about Bentell. I am eager to meet him and become his student." Essa then led me out of the teeming marketplace to the shade of a neem tree. He sat on the ground and motioned for me to sit near him. I made myself comfortable. "Bentell is a powerful mystic, but there is much that I myself do not understand," I answered. "In many ways I don't know him at all.

"What else?" He looked unwaveringly into my eyes, totally present. A trace of a smile lit his relaxed face.

"He has an intense love of life." I chose my words very carefully.

"What else?" Essa asked again.

"Just that he's a mystery.

"No one has been able to tell me much about him. I will have to see for myself," Essa exclaimed with a twinkle in his eye.

"There is one thing that Bentell instructed me to tell you. He said we should be very careful since this would be a dangerous trip. He said our lives would depend on staying aware and keeping alert.

"What kind of danger was he referring to?

"I don't know, but I have never known Bentell to give warnings without reason.

"Does Bentell give warnings often?

"No. He seldom warned me about anything."

Essa stood and walked a few steps away from me. He stopped, turned back and said, "I am pleased that Bentell chose me to be his student. Thank you for being here to guide me through whatever unknown dangers we will face on this journey."

I told Essa we should purchase enough food for a week and leave the next morning at first light. Essa at once accepted my plans. I sensed that whatever the dangers, Essa was a person who loved life and said yes to the universe.

Early the next morning, we departed on our journey. Soon we had left the plains and were steadily climbing lush hills under the warm midday sun. Through the more densely forested parts we were always aware of the abundance of life. A low growl out of the darkness startled me. I thought it might be a tiger, but I controlled my fear. I believed then that my physical and spiritual training of several years, which I regarded as strenuous, had prepared me to face death at any moment. Yet in the deepest recesses of my heart the insidious fear clung, of the leopard that stalks, the snake that slithers, and the scorpion that ambushes. I constantly scanned the trees overhead and remained very much aware of the path I trod.

Essa followed closely behind me, remaining mostly silent, but occasionally expressing his joyful appreciation of the unspoiled nature all around us. He particularly liked to watch the monkeys in their high-flying acts atop the green canopy of the forest and the crimson-throated barbets that turned gracefully in the air, performing arches and arabesques around our heads. We walked through a long stretch of junipers and past various species of white and pink rhododendron. We paused while Essa attempted to make friends with a mongoose that had bravely approached us. We marched on, and the far mountains, clouds, and wide sky reflected the beauty of the day.

We quickly got used to each other. Essa remained mostly silent but was still easy to get along with. Now and then, Essa asked a question that revealed the depth of his meditation and his eagerness on the spiritual path.

"Tell me what your teacher taught you about truth and reality." Essa smiled, knowing that this was indeed more than just a casual request.

I felt a great responsibility to answer accurately, yet I felt some- what unqualified. I meditated a few minutes, as we walked on a stretch of gentle slope, and Essa mercifully accorded me all the time I needed. Then I answered: "Truth is what is. When we go behind the curtain of illusion and practice the presence of reality, then truth is seen. I think this is about what Bentell would say.

"Very well put." Essa nodded in approval and did not probe any further. The praise made me blush in embarrassment, but I took pleasure in his appreciation of my knowledge. I was totally charmed by Essa. Serious, smiling Essa.

We walked higher and higher into the mountainous section of northern India. We didn't see a house or any other sign of people. The trail was often marked only by a broken twig or a bent blade of grass.

The sun moved steadily upward in the blue sky. When it was overhead, we stopped in the shade of a large spruce tree for our daily meal. It felt good to rest after the day's march. We took out our supplies of locally grown vegetables, milk, berries, and a flat bread made with rice-meal. Essa shared with me in the preparation of our food.

We sat on a rock near the edge of a cliff, which served as a beautiful vantage point from which we marveled at the majestic views of the vast lowlands we had just traveled through. It was breathtaking. A great expanse in all shades of gold and green lay unrolled at our feet like a rich carpet from the Creator's own loom. A thin ribbon running westward and sparkling in the sun told of the river that would flood these fertile lands during the rainy season. The thatched roofs and mud walls of the villagers' huts blended so well in the palette of the great plain that whole villages were hardly distinguishable.

In the mountains, still above us, there were many patches of weeds, now sunburned so that they were ochre yellow on the gray rocks. I had always been in love with these mountains, and I never felt more content than just now, enjoying their beauty.

Essa had not yet tasted his food. Far below us a herd of elephants filed past, stopping here and there where clumps of bushes stood, to dine upon the leafy vegetation. Their huge lumbering bodies dwarfed everything in a strange play of perspective. Essa watched them, a look of great contentment upon his face. Finally he turned toward me and offered a short prayer of thanksgiving for our meal: "Thank you father for love and for food; thank you for Lamas and the beautiful land we travel. Most of all thank you for life."

I sprinkled salt on my bread and quickly wolfed down my food. I am tall and lanky and have a young man's appetite. Essa ate slowly, and I finished while his bowl was still almost full.

Now I felt awkward watching Essa slowly eat while I had no food left, so I started talking. "I will tell you a story of Bentell and the beautifully woven blanket I bought for him." Essa gave me his attention as he continued to eat. "When Bentell meditates, he often has a blanket wrapped around him. To show my love, I bought a new and expensive, intricately woven blanket for him. I was sure that this was the perfect present for me to give Bentell. It cost more than I could really afford, but how could I better express my appreciation and eternal gratitude of the master? I wanted something really fine.

"Some months before, I had picked a wild flower for him. He delighted for a long time over this simple little flower. It had become a habit of mine during my daily walks to bring back an offering from nature to my beloved teacher. There had been more flowers, passionately colored leaves, a strange piece of twisted wood, beautiful rocks. All were free and all absolutely delighted him. I could hardly wait to give Bentell this very beautiful and warm blanket that I had personally chosen and bought at some sacrifice. I eagerly anticipated his delight.

"I walked over to Bentell with the blanket under my arm. I attempted to put my love gift around him but he refused to allow this. He sternly told me to take the blanket away. He said that my choice of gift belonged on the worldly material plane. He did not want it and ordered me to give it away to someone else. I was utterly crushed and filled with despair."

Essa grinned knowingly as I completed the story.

"On my next trip to the nearby village, I gave the blanket to a beggar. In my poor choice of a gift, only my ego had benefited from the sacrifice of buying such an expensive blanket. It took many months before I totally regained my composure in front of Bentell, knowing that I need not carry the guilt of any wrongdoing. I abandoned the concepts of guilt and sacrifice. From this experience, I learned that a simple flower is more important to Bentell than the finest blanket money can buy."

An understanding smile spread across Essa's face.

I felt reassured by Essa's obvious approval of my story and by his keen attention, and I decided to probe him. "You yourself appear to be clear and spiritually advanced. Why is it that you decided to come and study with Bentell?"

Essa thought before he answered. "I know that I have progressed immeasurably in my quest for spiritual growth. Still there is a void within me that remains to be filled. All my life, some force attracted me toward a special teacher. Recently, I meditated and focused deeply on my future direction. I came to know that the special teacher I needed was Bentell. Soon afterward and quite mysteriously, a messenger came to tell me that Bentell invited me to be his student. I knew it was no coincidence that the invitation came when it did. Since then my purpose has been clear."

A wonderful friendship began between Essa and myself. After our meal we lingered at this beautiful spot while I explained Bentell's method of meditation. "All Bentell's students are required to meditate for one hour twice a day. Bentell says that meditation is the surest way to liberation from the control of our ceaseless thoughts. We just sit silently and watch our thoughts parade through our head," I said. "No matter how enticing any thought is, we treat it as just another thought and we do not become attached to it or give it any special significance. We simply allow thoughts to pass through us. As a result of sitting, the mind becomes still and focused. Sense perceptions become more refined. We see and hear things of which we were not aware before."

Even as I said this, I was aware that Essa had the aura of calmness of one who already practices meditation, but I continued anyway. "Thoughts are not really ours. They come to us from another person or from some universal energy that I do not yet understand. We then process these thoughts and mistakenly think that they belong to us. We then become controlled by these foreign thoughts."

Essa listened politely, but he already sat silently, naturally doing the things I still only talked about. I became silent and joined Essa in that other landscape of inner peace.

We had meditated only a few minutes when a distant noise caught my attention. At first this sound, like the others from the wilderness around us, quickly passed through my consciousness and away.

But unlike the others, this one kept returning. Each time it returned, it gained in magnitude and seemed to be closing in. I fancied the cheerful song of the birds changing subtly yet abruptly in to a warning of approaching danger.

Essa shared my awareness. "It sounds like a rather large group of people heading in our direction," he said.

I associated a strange sense of danger with the approach of the group. "Let's go back the way we came," I replied with apprehension in my voice. The only escape was back down the mountain.

"No, we can remain here. We need not fear unknown forces in life," Essa said calmly.

At times, I have the ability to know of certain events beforehand. I knew this to be an instance of my intuitive talent. The sound continued to get closer and louder. Suddenly from around the bend, a band of armed men approached. They carried swords and spears, but they were not soldiers. Their rough dress and bearing plainly showed they were dacoits, bandits who preyed on travelers. There were perhaps a dozen of them, and there was no doubt that we had been followed to this secluded and dangerous place.

The difficulty of our position became more evident. We had chosen a scenic lunch spot on the edge of a steep cliff. There was no way to flee. We were quite trapped with the bandits on one side and the cliff on the other. I recalled the stories of the savageness of roving bandit gangs. They often forced their presence upon a peaceful encampment of nomads, gorging themselves upon their food, slaughtering as much cattle as they wished, abusing the women, then leaving, loaded down with all they could steal. No one dared resist them. At times they even descended in raids upon isolated villages, breaking into and pillaging any outlying huts. Their grim fame included as well the stealing of children and their immense pleasure in torturing their victims to death.

Finally, their easiest prey remained a couple of lonely travelers like ourselves with nothing to barter for our lives. They often killed poor men who dared not to have anything of value to satisfy their greed. How stupid of Essa to refuse my earlier advice to flee. We were now in the hands of merciless killers. A large crow flew overhead and loudly squawked as if mocking our predicament.

One of the most fearsome looking of the bandits came forward and stopped twenty feet from us. He must have been their leader. He studied us a moment and with a long grunt, said, "You filthy bastards. Your lives are mine. If I wished it, I could kill you this very moment. Still, I won't kill you, if you pay me enough!" He roared in laughter, slapping his thighs and the others roared their agreement with similar great mirth. A cold fear crawled down my spine.

I glanced at Essa, standing to my left. Even his peace and tranquility were shattered with the threat. I could not believe the change that had come over him. The blood had drained from his face. His inner glow was extinguished. He looked astonished. His mouth opened and shut, but he didn't say anything. His body stiffened. His face was white. His fixed eyes betrayed his real fear. Essa must have finally realized that we had nothing to give the bandits and would be killed. I knew all hope was lost when I saw that Essa had started trembling.

This peaceful, majestic cliff suddenly turned into a sinister obstacle blocking our escape from a horrible death.

The leader was so close that I could see he had two swords in his belt as well as a bone-handled knife. His face was scarred heavily from past fights, and the old cuts stood out in ugly purplish zigzagging lines under all the dirt and grease that covered his weather-beaten skin. His long hair hung in oily mats behind his ears, one of which had half a lobe missing. He had an uneven sparse beard, which added to his generally disgusting appearance. He held dark unblinking eyes upon us, and try as I did, I couldn't see even the slightest trace of compassion in his hard cold face.

His bearing clearly was that of a powerful and arrogant fighter. I couldn't imagine anyone I would less like to meet. We should have tried to escape earlier, I kept thinking over and over. We could have hidden before the bandits saw us.

I looked at this wild beast of a man and then to gentle Essa, who I now saw as a man with very little sense. It was Essa's fault that we stopped in this unprotected place. Would my life have to end this way? Why did this have to happen to me? This was happening to me because I had put too much faith too soon in a stranger of whom I had been told wonders! I had neglected my own self-reliance and had depended on his judgment alone! Now he had led us into an impossible situation and he, too, was afraid! As fear breeds more fear, I now felt sheer terror envelop me. Sweat drenched my body and pearled on my forehead and neck. There was little time left to live. My mind raced wildly, calculating the odds. I had a small knife that I could reach. If I killed the leader we might escape in the confusion.

The bandit leader cleared his throat, drew back his head and spat in our direction. "Now! Get them now," he commanded and the bandits moved closer.

"Throw them over the cliff," yelled one of the thugs, his mouth a dark and toothless cave.

"No! Cut off their heads," barked the leader.

I was shaken to the very core of my being. Everything was absolutely hopeless. Metal scraped on metal as they drew their swords. The earth stood still and already mourned for those of us about to die.

And still I looked to Essa for direction. He shook his head once in obvious denial of the situation. But then he faced front again with a new intent.

How can I even begin to describe the speed with which everything changed? Essa was not only calm again, he was suddenly glowing from within, radiating the peaceful force that comes from a deep rejoicing in all existence. For a moment, all stood still. In that very moment, Essa picked a beautiful gold wildflower that he noticed growing at his feet. As I stood helplessly watching him, holding my breath for what seemed an eternity, Essa studied the little flower carefully, smelled it, touched it to his forehead, his lips, his heart. Then he walked straight to the leader of the dacoit gang, and offered it to him in its full glory.

I saw the swift anger in the bandit's eyes as he burst out, "How dare you offer me a mere flower. I want money. Don't you know who I am? I could slice off your head without even blinking an eye.

"Yes you could, and even as my own eyes blink in death, I would continue to shower you with love," replied Essa. "It is my only and most valuable treasure.

"If that's all you have then get out of my sight, you crazy man," mumbled the bandit leader. "Take your companion and run from here at once. Madmen!" he grumbled toward his companions, and shrugged his shoulders. Then turning toward us once more, he threw the little flower down, ground it into the earth with his heel, and spat upon it with great contempt. "Run," he roared, "before I make you share the same fate as this flower." I was astonished. This reaction was totally out of character with the reputation of these bandits.

I had been holding my breath in sheer terror and now gave an involuntary sigh of relief. It seemed as if a veil dropped and the secret spell had been broken. Still trembling, I followed Essa away from this death threat. An aura of calm surrounded him so that my own fear somewhat drained away. In a few minutes, we walked confidently ahead into the still unknown dangers and adventures.

We had hardly traveled any distance when there was a tremendous surge in Essa's life energy. The encounter with the bandits and the rarefied air at this altitude had exhausted my endurance. I had been painfully trying to keep up with Essa's brisk pace, step for step, but I felt more and more subject to a great lassitude. Now, as I became aware of this new level of energy emanating from his presence, and as I visualized myself equally absorbed in it, the weariness left my step as if gravity itself no longer existed. I easily matched Essa's quickening gait as we stepped forward.

During the following weeks, we marched on toward our destination. We traveled through deep dark forests, full with the lives of hundreds of wild creatures. These often led us to rich fertile valleys where we could count on pleasant villages, a good night's rest, and fresh provisions. Villagers often gathered around us as we came to the communal well or the river banks to draw water for a well-deserved bath. The women in long colorful woolen skirts adorned with long flying pieces of ribbon, cast furtive glances in our direction, unable as they were to abandon their tasks and join the children who unashamedly stared at us and pulled on our robes. The men who had remained in the village stared also but from a distance. All were obviously curious of Essa, his light skin and hair. We never met with any hostility from these gentle people, in their colorful dress. Many wandering monks and holy men passed this way and they welcomed all, hoping to bring the blessings of the One upon their modest dwellings. As we started climbing to higher altitudes, the forests became sparser, and eventually, we reached a vast desolate region of high plateaus. The sheer expanse still in front of us held many foreboding thoughts, not the least of which was the possibility of another encounter with roving bandits. But in the far distance, we could faintly distinguish the outline of a chain of tall mountains, their snowcaps buried deep in the cloud cover. Even from this far, they held promise of incomparable loveliness. A few days later, with the setting sun on our backs, we approached our goal, nestled deep in the great Himalayan mountains. We were now steadily climbing jagged cliffs and steep inclines.

Essa was not ready for what he saw next. We came around a sharp twist in the path, and a narrow deep gorge opened itself in front of us. On the opposite side, seemingly suspended against the flank of the mountain was a monastery that reminded one of some magical children's tale. The sun, low in the west, illuminated the building beneath orange clouds. It took on the appearance of some enchanted kingdom. The light ochre and rose walls and the turquoise roofs with slightly curved corners shimmered in the fading sunlight as if the last evening rays meant to play a game with our weary minds. As each small cloud temporarily shaded the valley, the monastery was absorbed into the rock, the still dark windows the only assurance that it was not all a mirage. In the darkness, the temple looked awesome, mystical, transfixed in timelessness, as indeed I knew it was. For at dusk everyone would be meditating in absolute silence. Essa knew at once that this was the destination toward which we had been traveling. With excitement and expectation, we hurried on, taking great chances at times on the narrow and difficult path that led us to the depth of the valley. There we found a clear and cold stream in which we quickly bathed and washed our hair in preparation for our entrance into the monastery. We arrived just as the sun dropped down behind the mountain range through which we had traveled.

The monastery was a large stone structure that was modest and unadorned. There were no villages or houses in the vicinity, only this solitary retreat. The entrance was already open, so we walked in.

And we entered another world. A great feeling of peaceful power permeated the air. There were low wooden benches against two of the walls, beneath great tapestries of abstract and mystical designs. Near the inner entrance, an enormous gleaming gong hung between the two raised bodies of lions carved in red cinnabar wood. Many thong sandals, the only foot covering allowed monks, were aligned in perfect order by the entrance. A large carpet covered most of the stone floor, the only sign of material comfort. Yet the hall in its utter simplicity was visually perfect. One recognized the touch of the Master through his impeccable taste, his desire to envelop any visitor with immediate and absolute perfection. As with every previous time that I had entered this hall, I recognized a peculiar quality to the light which I did not fully understand. It was now very dim, the candles had not yet been lit, yet the little light there was seemed to grow slowly but constantly, much as the dawn lights up a new day.

"Come closer," said an angelic little man standing just inside the entrance. "I have been expecting you." He was one of my favorite people at the retreat. During the years that I had lived there, I had learned much from this man and had grown especially fond of him.

"Greetings, father," I said. "I want to introduce you to someone."

"Hello, hello," he beamed. "I am so happy you have arrived. You have done well, Lamas. Bentell knows you are here. Hurry, hurry now and don't be late. I have arranged two large basins of water in the courtyard in expectation of your late arrival. Quick, go practice your ablutions and join him. You will find him in silent meditation. Be sure not to say anything until he speaks first. Just sit, sit down and meditate with him."

My teacher, Bentell, sat motionless in the center of his meditation room. His legs were crossed, his eyes were shut, and he was wrapped in a pure white robe. He was partially bald, but his remaining hair was long and white. It mingled with his white beard so that I could not distinguish where his hair ended or his beard began. The stone steps of the candle rack were filled with dozens of candles that lit up a most beautiful face. In his fine clear features, I saw an inner peace that beamed warmth directly to my heart. A tremendous surging power radiated from him and engulfed me. All my previous fatigue seemed to seep quietly out of me.

Bentell opened his unfathomable, light blue eyes and with a serene gesture of his hand he told us to sit. Without a word, we took positions on either side of Bentell and settled down on round pillows. My heart swelled with love and veneration for this exquisite master.

During my previous four years of study with Bentell, he had taught me to meditate sitting on this type of pillow. His meditation instructions had been to relax totally and watch the thoughts come and go. Eventually, this watching would free us from our delusions. Bentell had said that this was a proven method of liberating our spiritual consciousness. At first, my back ached and my stiff legs rebelled against the pain. This, combined with various itches, compelled me to scratch and move. But I persisted and soon my body ceased its resistance. Eventually, I learned to sit motionless for hours at a time.

Today's meditation was deeper and more powerful than any before it. I experienced lightness and had a sensation of floating freely into the great vastness of space. My mind became crystal clear; I became clarity.

In the presence of Bentell, I always felt very loving and whole. This time I felt absolutely radiant. I felt bathed with the auras of two spiritually powerful people. We all sat there. It seemed to me that a long time passed. It could have been a day or merely hours. Never before had I felt such peace.

Eventually, an attendant came and led us to a small chamber containing a long well-worn table. The attendant set three wooden bowls in front of each of us. He served us hot bean soup, cooked rice, vegetables and cool milk. I realized I was starved. Yet I had no difficulty waiting a few moments longer while Bentell led a small prayer of thanks for our safe journey and our food. My enormous appetite surprised me, but perhaps it was a sign we had indeed meditated a long time.

We finished the meal and wiped out the bowls with pieces of bread. We ate the bread and placed the clean bowls upside down in readiness for future meals. We attended to our other personal needs and returned to be with Bentell. I had thought that by now Bentell would speak to us. But again we sat in silence, and again there was nothing to do but meditate.

The meditation was even more ecstatic than before. Still something in me hoped Bentell would say something. But it was not to be. Bentell never spoke.

Again we ate and then again meditated. Once, after one of our frugal meals, Essa whispered to me that approximately four days had past. Still Bentell had not parted his lips.

I had never before known Bentell to remain silent so long. Often he said things that I was not yet ready to hear. At those times, I had wished he were more silent. But now that I wanted to hear his beloved voice, he would not speak. On the seventh day, my desire for Bentell to speak had faded. By now my mind became as clear as a mountain stream. I had long ago stopped speculating about what Bentell would say. When I sat, I just sat. In my stillness, I witnessed everything.

Suddenly, when I no longer expected it, Bentell began to talk. He caught me completely by surprise. One moment I was deep in meditation, and the next I was hearing Bentell's perfect voice, yet I could not tell where the silence had left and the speech had begun. He addressed Essa.

"My son, I sent for you to travel here, to me, so that you may repay the visit we made at your birth. He spoke in a low voice that did not fit his powerful presence. Yet Bentell's voice was very loving and sent joy through my body. "You have reached almost the highest understanding. When I sent for you, there were seven teachings you needed in order to become total. These are seven levels of human experiences that, all with breath in their nostrils, must pass through. Passage through these seven levels is a necessary preparation for you to completely fulfill your destiny."

Bentell stood and moved over to Essa and sat down directly in front of him. Bentell put one hand on Essa's shoulder. His grip was firm yet gentle. He looked into Essa's eyes and continued speaking. "Even as you journeyed here, your first teaching was given by our notorious bandits. You learned that you must live with the knowledge that physical death is our constant companion and will occur before we know it. We are all going to face physical death. Instead of being paralyzed by the fear of death, you remembered the limitless possibilities of life. Rather than becoming stilted by the concept that you were about to die, you remembered that you were alive. You realized every moment is a new celebration of life. You became free to see the flowers at your feet, and to live."

With those last words, his voice lowered and he stopped speaking, and again there was a profound silence. I felt an intense reverence toward this gentle shining man. For as he praised Essa for remaining joyfully in the present rather than fearing the future—however immediate and fatal that future may seem—he also showed me how I had clung to the past in my anger and disappointment toward Essa. I had blamed him inwardly for our predicament. In fact, he had saved my life as well as his own through a minimal act of stupendous faith. Bentell slowly put his hand on Essa's head. His movements were balanced and graceful. Bright rays of blue-white light seemed to wash over Essa's body. Some unexplainable quality was being transmitted to Essa through the Master.

Suddenly, Bentell again began to speak as if he had never stopped. "Strange things will happen to you during your stay with us.

"What sort of things," asked Essa?

"That, Essa, depends on you," replied Bentell. "Your journey toward your destiny has already begun. Even now your second teaching is awaiting you. As you face it, remember to be quiet inside. Rejoice! The universe is yours if you just rejoice.

"Tomorrow you will leave the monastery in search of your next adventure. The priests at the temple of Jagannath know the secrets of the Vedas and how to use the power of these secrets."

Bentell stood and walked toward the door. He paused at the doorway, turned around to face us, and delivered a departing remark: "Journey south toward the temple of Jagannath at Puri near the Bay of Bengal in eastern India. I have arranged for you to stay in the holy temple. There you will be given the second of the seven levels of teachings. If you allow your minds to be open and free, then at Jagannath this teaching will be of great value.

"Have confidence that I will go before you and make the crooked places straight. Sleep now, for the night is short, and the sun will soon rise."

18 The Messiah In India

Chapter II

SEXUALITY

After three weeks of continuous walking, my legs ached and my body was weary. I thought my lot in life was to travel from here to there, and I lost all awareness of distances. Placing one foot in front of the other became a monotonous mechanical occupation, yet it also became a kind of meditation. Walking emptied my mind more fully than Bentell's breath meditation. All thought of my desires and troubles ceased as I concentrated almost totally on where I placed my feet. Up and down the hills and through the dense forest we walked. At times, our way became a narrow twisting maze-like path between ancient birch and fir trees. I pulled my hood down hard on my head and walked some more.

Essa and I walked on slowly but steadily along the primitive winding path, doggedly climbing toward the temple of Jagannath. As I walked, I remembered stories of Jagannath and wondered what great teachings we would gather there. Jagannath, which means Lord of the Universe, was said to be the world's most glorious temple, rich in beauty and culture, and to have a vast library of ancient spiritual wisdom. Here were said to dwell hundreds of priests, yogis, and sages, who possessed the extraordinary powers of the Vedas.

Mile after mile, we walked. By mid morning, the sun was quite hot and I felt it on the back of my neck, causing sweat to trickle down my back. We eagerly stopped at a watering hole and found immediate relief in its cool waters. We walked on into a great expanse of rolling fields, filled with the tall spires of gold flowers gently swaying to and fro in the warm breeze. Here and there a clump of blue hibiscus bloomed like a spot of brilliant evening sky mirrored upon a golden pond. Finally, Essa and I came to a hilltop from which we were able to discern faintly upon the horizon the tall steeples of the Temple of Jagannath still many miles off in the distance, and with renewed vigor we resumed our walk toward it. As we slowly approached the temple, my heart beat quickly in expectation of its great wonders.

The massive main structure of the temple stood on elevated ground and was surrounded by innumerable smaller temples and shrines, disseminated in an immense park-like area, itself enclosed by a twenty-foot high wall.

We drew near to the east wall and approached a number of guards who stood outside the gate. Essa spoke softly to the guards: "We are guests of the Rajah of Puri. Please take us to him."

One guard led the way through the gate toward the main temple. We walked through the huge rectangular gate, then for a moment stood in silent awe at the magnificence of the entrance hall. There were sunken courtyards with shimmering pools and a marbled pathway, hedged with luxuriant tropical vegetation that led to quiet coves nestled in evergreens. We proceeded through this inner sanctuary and passed by a pleasing rock formation splashed with the colors of a flowering vine. Here in a quiet niche, a devotee, enveloped in long matted hair, was deep in meditation, his eyes as limpid as the water itself.

The guard wanted to hurry and get to the main inner temple, but Essa first wanted to explore another adjacent garden, this one filled with a thousand and one species of exotic plants. We paused a moment and Essa pointed to some large glossy leaves, heart-shaped and dashed with purple stripes. I slowed down my mind trying to view the garden through his conscious eyes. The breeze rose gently as we tarried for a while among the precious plants.

We entered the inner temple, and the guards led us through a long dimly lit corridor, up stone steps, and to a very large chamber that was set up as a banquet hall. There they left us alone. I stood still and breathed deeply. The air was filled with sandalwood incense, and its smoke lay in still delicate layers, cloud-like, throughout the room.

We had only lingered in the banquet hall a few minutes when the Brahman priests arrived. Intrigued by the stories they heard of the powers concentrated in Essa, the priests showed their eagerness to delight us. They introduced themselves. There were at least a hundred of them, and they were divided into a dozen orders and classes.

The room quieted as a special priest entered. He was dressed in the traditional saffron dhoti, but his was richly inlaid in a gold pattern, a mark of great distinction. He bore a sandalwood paste dot on his forehead and was a tall man with an austere countenance. On his chest, an ornately jeweled star hung from a heavy silver chain in an intricate snake pattern.

They called him the Rajah, the head priest, and as he walked toward us, the other priests stepped aside in deference. His voice was deep and strong. "I am the Rajah of Puri! Welcome to Jagannath." His lips were two thin lines, but his jaw was strong and willful. Distinguished streaks of grey marbled his black hair, revealing the years of studies, the endless quest for always greater wisdom. In an instant his clear golden eyes had looked into the depth of my heart, and now he turned to look at Essa and said: "Essa and Lamas, I give you the honorary rank of priest. You will be treated with the utmost respect. My priests will make your stay a happy and productive one."

Essa replied, "Thank you for being so generous. I am eager to learn Hinduism from you."

The Rajah of Puri smiled and continued: "Hinduism is our religion, philosophy, and way of life. It dates back to prehistoric times and is the first religion given to man. There are many scriptures of Hinduism, all of which you will have an opportunity to study. Over one thousand years ago, the Vedas, our first sacred literature, was written down. It is composed of four ancient collections of sacred hymns and prayers and reveals the most sacred truths that can be known to man. This body of knowledge always existed, and the ancients transmitted it orally from generation to generation before the invention of writing.

"My students find it necessary to study diligently for many years before developing a good understanding of its true significance. You may study at your own rate, and my priests will assist you whenever you request. You are indeed fortunate to study here, because only we Brahman priests have a unique and direct connection to God and have knowledge of the wisdom you seek."

The Rajah priest led us to a long table loaded with several varieties of curry, chutneys, raitas, choice fruit juices, pieces of tender coconut, pomegranates, guavas, and other delicacies. Some of these foods we had never sampled before. We all bowed our heads, and the Rajah priest blessed the food and the God who brought us abundant life.

We sat, and servants set banana leaves in front of us and placed portions of these foods on them. The priests chanted a prayer of thanksgiving and began to eat. I picked up a strange spongy food with a pungent smell. I ate it, and it was quite spicy but I remained unsure of what I was eating. Both Essa and I temporarily modified our eating habits to fit in with the local customs. The priests' food was either too sweet or dominated by hot, unfamiliar spices. One singular rectangular morsel left a numb feeling in my mouth that lingered for many uncomfortable minutes. Eating these strange foods was difficult for me. Still, I remained humble and sampled everything served to us.

Several times during the meal, the Rajah of Puri intently observed Essa. "Essa," he inquired, "you are not like other men, and you come from far away. What is the place you call home?

"I come from a land across the Arabian Sea." Essa smiled warmly at the high priest as he did with almost everyone. Seeing the high priest's eyebrows rise in consternation, he went on, "It is many hundreds of miles west of here and even further away in the difference of customs."

Essa, as usual, enjoyed himself. He was in high spirits and kept the priests amused with his clever wit. Though he obviously meant to take all aspects of life seriously, Essa usually took himself lightly. The banquet table was alive with the laughter of the priests when Essa told a story of the blind leading the blind. They delighted in his anecdote of the wolves in sheep's clothing. Essa was clearly in control of the situation. He combined analytical thought with the spontaneity of a free child.

I remained rather quiet and watched Essa place the priests under his spell. Essa spoke with a quality of authority that the priests had never before seen in a man of his youth, and they listened intently. Even the Rajah of Puri spoke with a borrowed authority from other sources. Essa spoke with his own authority.

When dinner ended, the Brahmans, Essa, and I all left in good spirits. An old priest led Essa and me outside to our individual rooms in a building adjacent to the main temple. My room there was much bigger than even my parent's entire house, and it opened onto a tiny veranda filled with fragrant flowering vines. In a corner, a small fountain spouted a rivulet onto the turquoise mosaic floor and around potted flowers. Near the ceiling, in a large round white and gold cage, a pair of brightly plumed exotic birds slept peacefully on their perch, close together. I stared for a few minutes at the walls, which were decorated with elaborate paintings of various deities in all manners of sexual intercourse. The paintings piqued my curiosity, but our long day on the road made the richly appointed bed seem even more appealing. I removed my robe and lay back on the soft cushions of silk and brocade.

In these idyllic surroundings, I soon drifted into a dream-like state, only to be jolted awake by an irritating knock at the door. A priest entered, followed by a young woman of rare beauty. I quickly stood up, pulling my robe around me. "His Holiness, the Rajah of Puri, requests that you be made comfortable," said the priest. Then he immediately introduced the young woman to me and told me she would tend to all my needs.

"What was that?" I muttered. I couldn't believe what I heard and felt, in my half-dressed state, more embarrassed than attractive.

"She will tend to all your needs," he repeated, with the slightest hint of a smile on his face.

I thought I knew what he meant, but I still could not be sure. I hoped for a further explanation or at least another clue, but he volunteered nothing else.

All my needs. With my senses aroused by the sensuality of the atmosphere all around, my mind momentarily flashed upon the sexual scenes on the walls. In that very moment, the old priest had left. His heavy steps rang out on the stones, then softened in the distance. Now I became aware of the stimulating fragrance of perfume, and the hormones of my manhood raced throughout my body.

Lelia was her name. She was only sixteen and had been reared in the temple for the last twelve years. She had been given to the temple by her parents to be consecrated to God. Here, she was well educated in the tantric art of sexual yoga worship and other skills that were necessary for her esteemed position. She knew that she was in the temple for a holy purpose, so she joyfully strived for the perfection of her mind and body. She had been closely supervised in her mental and physical development. Her diet consisted of a special balance of food designed to benefit her training.

She was delightful. She gracefully massaged my sore feet, while sitting on her heels in front of me, digging her knuckles deep. Sometimes pressing with her thumbs in certain patterns, deeply breathing out, she caused entire areas of my body to release their tension and aches, and soon I felt renewed in body and spirit. Now, she tenderly caressed my ankles and, for a finishing touch, she lightly kissed the instep of both feet. I loved the sensuous pleasure of it. I lay down and she placed her hands on my back and kneaded my sore muscles with the skill of a masseuse. She was the most attentive woman I had ever known. I rolled onto my back and looked into her eyes. She slowly brought her face closer to mine until our lips met. Her long and glistening dark hair uncoiled itself and softly caressed my neck.

I surrendered and closed my eyes. She started scratching my skin ever so lightly, and presently she made a soft purring sound in her throat, exhaling as her nails reached down across my belly and down to my thighs. Then she breathed in again, slowly and fully, her hands flat this time, climbing back to my shoulders, not quite touching my skin but slightly removed from my body on either side. Now she scratched me again, a little harder and the purring sound became a little more of a growl. Her moves became more and more a hypnotic dance. She pulled me to her, enveloping me into her aura. I burned with desire.

She blow out the light, the night, the time. Completely enraptured, I held her in embrace. I was under her skin, inside her arms and chest and lower back, strocking each nerve ending. I was in her bones and skull and behind her eyes, and she moaned the strange and beautiful sounds of love. All through the night, Lelia taught me to burn with the exalted joy of sex. True to the high priest's promise, she tended to all my needs.

The next morning, I awoke early and left my lovely sleeping mate to find Essa. When we stayed as guests in a monastery or a caravansarai, Essa usually meditated outdoors early each morning, so I walked into the garden. All night it had rained heavily and now, in the fast-warming air of the morning, a soft mist rose from the landscaped grounds. Overhead, silver and green leaves glistened in the sun, heavy water drops hanging from their rounded edges like crystals and sapphires. Some of them dripped onto me, but it mattered little. The garden was most peaceful and enchanting. I walked slowly to inhale the fragrance of the many flowers. A butterfly delicately poised on a twig allowed me to reach up and capture it. I studied the delicate patterns on its multi-colored wings. I opened my hand and the butterfly hesitated as if studying me, then flew gracefully away.

I was blissful and desired to share my feelings with Essa, but I couldn't find him. I searched through the entire garden, but still I couldn't locate him. Instead I found the Raja of Puri and asked him about Essa's whereabouts. The Raja said, "Essa had an exhausting night, is sleeping late, and is not to be disturbed. I will personally escorted you to the study hall to begin your reading of the sacred Veda scrolls."

We left the beautiful gardens of the inner temple for another building—he archives pavilion, a perfectly square stone edifice. A stone patio, separated from the garden by a delicately sculptured archway, held the constant traffic of barefooted monks, pacing back and forth and around, pondering some fine philosophic points of the Vedas. Here the silence was only disturbed by the faintest swishing sound of the priests' white or saffron dhotis. Everywhere the patio stones had been worn smooth and shiny by the Brahmans' steps. I diligently studied scrolls all day, reading various sutras, written in Devanagiri script, until late in the evening. Essa never joined me.

The next day I returned to the archives and resumed my studies. I was lost in my reading of the beautiful scriptures when the Raja entered, smiled at me, opened a cloth bag, and extracted a manuscript. "You will be interested in reading this," he said. "It is an eyewitness account of an unusual conception. The reason for our interest is the report that your companion Essa is said to have been conceived in exactly this manner." He smiled again and left.

The manuscript was copied on new cloth and appeared to have been written within the last few years. I picked it up, somewhat apprehensive at the realization that it might be the story of my friend's conception. Not knowing what to expect, I started reading.

The full moon periodically appeared from behind its veils of clouds like an intruder trying to catch a glimpse of the ceremony that had now just begun. It was exactly midnight and a small group of people had gathered on the sacred hilltop.

Bright firelight danced on the figures of twelve men. On very rare occasions, during times of spiritual transition, it was their custom to create a mutual child.

The child would be conceived during this special ceremony. This ceremony would also unify the powerful leaders of the ancient Essene sect. The mystically conceived child would be related to all those present. Gathered here in an act of absolute love, they would bring their life forces together. Their shared energy would create life itself. They would father a very special child. Their souls would unite with the universal spirit and incarnate.

They would father The Son.

The twelve men sat in a circle. Each looked out and saw the other. They sat silent and still and shared their spiritual energy with the circle. This circle completed a mystic circuit that resulted in a tremendous magnification of the total energies within it.

The twelve men concentrated on a powerful meditation technique called circular breathing. Their exhalation and inhalation were connected in one continuous, circular, soft breathing cycle. This special breathing increased the spiritual energy within each and the whole of them. As their individual energies grew, they shared them with the complete circle. Their mutual energies surged back and forth between them in rhythm to their breathing. They participated fully and gave with total commitment. Slowly and inexorably, they became one being.

The clouds of the evening had disappeared behind the distant hills and ridges that encircled this secret gathering place, and now all the stars in heaven illuminated the scene.

The breathing lasted two hours. Then they rose and began chanting the various Holy Names. Turning their faces to the firmament, opening their arms wide, gyrating slowly in place, they became themselves another constellation. The red glow of the fire reflected the determination in their faces. They surrendered themselves to a state of sacredness, one by one and collectively. There was a sense of anticipation and excitement. Their bodies moved and swayed to some mysterious force.

Kneeling on an altar inside this circle was the virgin bride. For her, this was a great honor. She was specially selected for her high moral character and her spiritual qualities. Like the twelve men, she was also deep in her own chanting, her eyes fixed on the high moon.

Also inside the circle was an old sage woman. She was a powerful female elder who was chosen to be the mistress of ceremonies. The success or failure of this entire ritual rested in the hands of this sage woman. She was aware of the importance of every act she performed, and her concentration was total.

The old woman comforted and encouraged the virgin with words of reassurance. Now she moved to the perimeter of the circle. The circle was marked out by twelve staffs. Each of the men came to sit in front of a staff. All twelve men were chosen to provide exceptional human qualities for the son they would soon father. One of the males was chosen for intelligence, and his pattern represented this quality. Another man's pattern stood for spiritual love, and so on.

The old woman picked up her scepter of power in her right hand and approached one of the men. She touched him lightly on the head with the scepter and instructed him on how to improve his special quality. She spoke in a whisper, very close to his ear: "Allow your quality of loving forgiveness to take over your consciousness so that you are completely filled and fully identified with loving forgiveness."

The old woman walked slowly around the circle, speaking individually with each man, then moved back toward the virgin and touched her on the head with the scepter.

The old woman spoke loudly. "The Infinite Spirit alone has existed from eternity. He composes the one and only indivisible soul of the universe. He alone creates and animates the whole. He is the cause of the mysterious life of man, in whom He has breathed a part of His Being. He willed the earth and heavens to be created. Here tonight, He will create again."

The men began chanting again, their chant gaining in power and intent. An eerie din of chants and incantations became far more than the whole chant of the twelve men. Spirit itself had joined the mystical ceremony.

The old woman walked slowly around the virgin seven times while the chanting continued. At times, the chants ebbed, but only to renew themselves even greater. The fire pulsated to the higher and higher frequencies of energy that were being created.

The distant rumble of thunder was heard first from one direction, then another, sustaining the men's chants, answering them, colliding against them. The air itself became heavy and full of vibrations, full of unknowable mysteries.

The ceremony approached a climax. All the men were now in a supernatural frenzy. The old woman picked up the sacred cup to begin the grand finale. It was called a shofar and was actually a hollow horn taken from the head of a special ram. It was slightly curved and highly waxed and had a large opening at one end and a small opening at the other. The old woman danced back in a hypnotic sway, to the circle of the men. She held high the sacred cup and demanded that each male focus consciousness on his quality of God.

One of the males chanted: "I thank God and celebrate the glory of life. I love and am loved. I am one with all."

The old woman lowered the sacred cup and it now served as a shofar. She put the small opening to her lips and blew so that a loud, beckoning sound was emitted from the large opening. This holy horn announced the last and most crucial part of the ceremony.

As the sage woman brought the shofar down again, a lightning bolt tore the heavens, and the earth shook once, but none of the participants wavered even an instant in their concentration.

The old woman sealed the small opening of the shofar with the palm of her left hand and offered the large opening to one of the males. The horn now served as the sacred cup. The holy man totally centered his consciousness on becoming one with his particular embodiment of God. Now in a frenzied state he shouted his chant. "I am a living branch, one with the tree. I am the tree being one with me. I am one with all." His vital life force came forth and flowed into the large end of the sacred cup.

The old woman quickly made her rounds, similarly collecting the life force from the other males, as lightning bolts struck here and there, setting the darkened sky afire. This life-force was brought forth not from the humans present, but from the Infinite Spirit. This force represented the material embodiment of the Eternal Being.

The last male made his contribution and the old woman raised her sacramental cup triumphantly.

The rising sun began to break over two distant peaks, swiftly dispelling the dark clouds and adding its illuminating presence to the ceremony. The old woman hurried over to the still-chanting virgin bride and again held up the sacred cup. She had the virgin recline and held the cup over her womb. She began her chant:

"Fathered by the one.
The perfection of love, harmony and beauty.
The only being.
We are united with all the illuminated souls
Who form the embodiment of the master,
The spirit of guidance."

The narrow portion of the ram's horn was given to the virgin. The old woman put her face to the large opening and blew with all her force. All eternity paused as the God spirits of all twelve males rushed forth together to inseminate the virgin.

As the sun rose in the east, the Son was created.

It was late in March, and life was beginning to flourish. Everywhere, thorn hedges already light green with new buds, silently celebrated the beginning of spring. Their beautiful vigor for life demonstrated their victory over the recent deadness of winter.

The ceremony was timed to produce a child during the most promising of the upcoming astrological signs. The birth would coincide with an especially powerful event, a rare occurrence of three sets of multiple planetary conjunctions in the constellation of Pisces. This sign would be all the more important since it was now a transitory period at the beginning of the Piscean Age. This was a powerful time in which there would be many changes in the order of things.

The sun was dazzling now and clear of the distant mountains, bathing everyone in its radiance. The dye was cast. The chanting of the participants slowly faded away. They left their positions in the circle and mingled with each other. They hugged and exchanged greetings of pleasure. They celebrated with gestures of joy, for they knew they had done all that was possible to transfer their spirit to flesh. The rest was in the hands of God.

I put the manuscript down, stunned! I sat there not knowing what to believe. Was Essa really conceived in such a special way, and if so, what did it mean? I had to ask Essa. I quickly located the Raja at the other end of the archives and again asked to see Essa. But again the Raja said Essa was not to be disturbed.

"What do you think of the unusual conception?" I asked the Raja.

"We don't know," he answered. "Because of this manuscript, we have opened our great temple to you both, but we're not sure if we believe this extraordinary story. And yet. " The Raja smiled with his thin lips, departed from the archives and left me with many still unanswered questions. There was nothing to do but reread the document and hope for an explanation.

Another day passed without Essa. I began to fear for his safety, so I again inquired of the Raja of Puri. Soon afterward, Essa sheepishly joined me in the archives and said, "Lamas my good friend, how are you? Everything is perfect with me and I have so much to tell you.

"And I have much to ask," I replied, and went on to tell about the manuscript that I read. "Is it true? Were you really conceived in a sacred ceremony?"

For a long moment there was no reply, then Essa looked off in the distance and said, "It is something I cannot discuss with you now.

"Well, just tell me if it was about you.

"Enough of that manuscript for now. Let me tell you what has happened to me during the last few days." I was surprised and upset that Essa would not trust me with a straight answer, but I could see that probing him further would remain futile. I was determined to discover if Essa was really one of the children created by the Essene ceremony, but I would wait patiently for a better time to ask him again.

Essa told me that he had also been presented with a woman. The woman offered to Essa was well educated and eager to please. She was soft in appearance and had a smile that was both shy and provocative. As she walked into the room, Essa's eyes momentarily dwelt on the sweet curve of her lips. She was short and slender, young looking, yet her figure and moves exuded both fulness of life and a certain maturity. Her long glistening black hair hung all the way down to the small of her back. Dark mysterious eyes sparkled with the excitement of life and sent forth vibrations of pure beauty. Her gold-colored skin radiated a sensual attraction that stirred deep desires in Essa. She was wrapped in several lengths of transparent veils that both accentuated and masked her appealing figure.

"My name is Panya," she said to Essa in a soft inviting voice that matched her look, "and I am very honored to be here." She played seductively with a fan made of peacock feathers.

"May his blessings shower upon you," said Essa. He felt unsure of himself in this situation, but he masked his inner doubts from Panya. At times, Essa experienced very strong sexual urges, yet he had never had a sexual relationship with a woman. Now he desperately wanted to touch her and learn the secrets of woman.

The small bells on Panya's ankles tinkled as she moved seductively closer to Essa. He became aware of both the faint music from the raga, playing across the garden in the marble and gold music pavilion, and the heady-sweet jasmine perfume of the night. It seemed as if Panya had brought this whole delicate ambience as she walked in with her swaying steps. Essa sat mesmerized in the presence of her being. Panya's steps had now become a slow and subtle dance. Still holding her fan in one hand, one moment she bowed to Essa, one moment she retreated in quickened steps across the room and turned away only to glance at him over her shoulder with dark smouldering eyes. Throughout her dance, in the midst of turns, slow circles where her naked feet seemed to barely graze the floor, graceful arabesques and the soft waving of her arms, she simply unwrapped one veil after another until she stood facing him. Her breasts were bare and slightly moist in the heat of the night and from her exertions. A richly jeweled girdle lowered on her stilled hips, from which one last pure white veil gathered in soft pleats, revealing her nakedness. The exquisite tinkling of the many little silver bells on Panya's ankles and garter had become one with the raga from the distant music pavilion. Now Panya kneeled at his feet and extending her beautifully curved arms in front, grazed his chest with her nails, making circles around his nipples, which were small and hard.

Intoxicated, transported by her dance, her beauty, and the purity held in the act of offering of herself, Essa almost allowed his last inner doubts to be swept away as he recalled Bentell's voice repeating: "There is just One Power. Desires of the flesh are only appearances of power and have no real power over you when you remember the One Power. Other powers only exist when you forget that there is only One Power."

Essa stood up and pulled Panya up gently by the wrists, but she freed herself and took one step back, setting the bells of her anklet and garter once more into sweet stimulating music. But Essa was firm and refused to surrendered to his desires. He had watched her whole dance, mesmerized but also respectful of the many years of training behind her art form. Now he lowered his eyes and distanced himself inwardly.

"What is wrong? she asked tenderly, but with worry in her voice. "Why the sudden change? Do I fail to some way to please you?

"No, your dance has pleased me immensely," replied Essa.

"Is something wrong between us, Essa? I beg of you, answer my questions. I must know what I have done to displease you.

"Panya, I don't want to pain you in any way. I have taken a vow of celibacy, and I shall not break it.

"Essa, if you do not let me stay, I will be disgraced and sent out from the temple in shame! Please at least let me stay here in your room.

"Essa please, I would even be willing to sleep on the floor."

Without answering or saying another word, Essa bowed his head, turned and walked out to the garden to meditate by himself. But Panya's words continuously occupied all his thoughts. Many hours later, after Panya had left Essa returned to his room and soon drifted into an uneasy sleep.

Essa awakened to the morning, already lit brightly by the warm sun high in the pure blue sky. Drawing up the silk coverlet to shut out the brightness, he lay silently and wondered, still somewhat nervous, about what to expect in this first day of his new studies. To be certain, Bentell must have known that Panya would be part of his experiences in this temple. Had not Bentell promised, "I will go before you and make the crooked places straight?" Yet Bentell had also said many times: "Rejoice! The Universe is yours if you only rejoice!" His vow of celibacy had been taken long before he had put himself under Bentell's loving guidance. Was it still truly valid? Or was it a rigid belief system that would keep him from his full destiny? Essa then began his studies in a private meditation hall but instead of concentrating on the Vedas he continued to struggle with this dilemma.

When next I saw Essa, he sat next to me and joined in the study of the sacred Vedas. The Rajah of Puri himself joined us in discussing their secrets. But Essa's participation in this discussion was lacking. It was apparent that Essa could not concentrate on his studies. His mind was on Panya; he was obsessed with the conflict of his desires and his celibacy. Something had changed in him. He could neither eat nor sleep.

Unlike Essa, I was not new to the ways of sexual love. Consequently, passion didn't take control of my thoughts the way it did with Essa. I studied the scrolls and would have been happy except for my concern about Essa. He behaved in a way that was very human, but not very spiritual.

The Rajah and his priests worked with Essa to teach him to read and understand the Vedas, the Holy Scriptures of the temple. However, they were aware of Essa's sexual obsession somewhat perplexed and annoyed that Essa did not share eagerly in the study of the mystic Vedas and instead spent all of his time on mere sexual pursuits. Celibacy was not prized by the priests, but the compulsive actions of this young Essa did not at all live up to the Rajah's expectations. Still, the Rajah knew the virtue of patience and allowed Essa to continue with his passion.

It's all too easy for things to go wrong. As the days became weeks, Essa realized that he had devoted too little time to his spiritual studies.

For now he realized that if thoughts of physical love devoured him, then Essa's dream of fulfilling his destiny would then remain unfinished.

The erotic spell weakened, and Essa's other interests revived in great intense flashes of awareness. Once you awaken to the truth, you can never really go back to sleep. You can nap, of course, but you always reawaken. You eventually stop dreaming. So it was with Essa.

Essa realized that the anticipation of Panya's body was more delicious than the actual possession. It was the desire for something, and not the actual having, that had driven him repeatedly to Panya's side. As his desires began to weaken, the entire universe called even more loudly for Essa to return to his path, but what would he say to Panya or to Bentell?

Essa sat by himself under a large mango tree and watched the ants carrying away bits of fruit. With his finger he wrote on the soft ground. Essa willed a solution to his dilemma, but none came. Hours passed in this state. Then his thoughts gave way to a vivid alertness. Essa was at once aware of everything, and all was different.

He realized who he really was. Essa remembered he had a destiny far beyond his temporary life with Panya. He imagined the voice of Bentell softly speaking and telling him what he must do. He knew he had been under the spell of carnal love. His path was to rise above sexual unions. It wasn't that sex itself was destructive. Rather, it was Essa's attachment to sex that would get in the way of his spiritual growth. For this very reason Bentell had not lifted his vow of celibacy but in fact averted the subject entirely. Now Essa knew that the pure love of all life was a higher path to which he was called. He was now freer than ever. He would never again view women in the same way he had before.

With a voice of conviction that I had not heard for weeks, Essa said to me, "Prepare to travel. I cannot read the Vedas here. We will soon leave this temple."

Essa received an audience with the Rajah of Puri and told him of our pending departure. The Rajah spoke of his disappointment with Essa's sexual obsession and of Essa's failure to study from the great spiritual writings. He no longer felt the same awe toward Essa and was eased in knowing that Essa was leaving of his own accord.

As we packed our blankets, I slowly became aware of the presence of Bentell. I turned and there he was. He stood only a few feet from Essa. In great surprise, Essa exclaimed, "Bentell! Where did you come from?

"I knew you would be wanting to see me now, so here I am." Bentell's always soothing voice seemed to come from everywhere at once.

"Bentell, Where did I go wrong?" asked Essa.

There was a typically long period of silence while Bentell looked partly amused and partly compassionate. Then he replied, "Life's dramatic joys and sadnesses are just teachings that free our consciousness to rise upward in further growth. Accept what you are. Accept that you are spirit born into form. In form, it is our nature to be sexual beings.

"It was necessary for you to experience sexual desire. In denying your sexuality you would have stored these desires in the deep recesses of your being. If you had suppressed sexual desire, only because of a vow made to another teacher long ago, your energies would have become stuck at this level. Now this vow is truly your own chosen path."

Bentell's voice was kind and clear. "Then your growth would have stopped. You could have remained frozen in this level all your life. Sex is a powerful force and it can block your rising energies." Essa, who usually sat almost motionless, now squirmed and adjusted his posture.

"Sex doesn't have to be seen as an enemy. If you accept sexual desire, then the conflict disappears. So don't make a choice. Instead, include sex in your awareness and transform sex by remaining present. Sexual energy is an attraction bringing love between individuals. Convert this sexual energy into a positive loving energy bringing love to your relationship with the One Spirit. Allow free movement to these transformed energies. Let them flow upward toward your natural evolution. Everything in the infinite universe sounds a note in the wonderful harmony of the mystery of your existence."

Bentell continued: "You did well to become aware and not to remain attached to those desires. Sensual desire becomes lust, lust becomes delusion, and delusion is the daydream of the world. Then, lives are not lived, but instead acted out in delusionary dreams. Pleasures of the senses can distract and enslave you. True pleasure comes from practicing the presence and living in the moment," continued Bentell. "Neither pleasure nor pain, or loss or gain are important. Take no thought of these transient dreams.

"Now that you have awakened from these dreams, you can clearly see that the rewards of sensual pleasure are but momentary.

True happiness goes far beyond these passing pleasures, and true happiness lasts forever. This realization is more important than the mere repetitive study of ancient scrolls.

"You have successfully learned the mystery of your second teaching, but five higher teachings await you. Now it is time to leave this temple and travel to the city of Benares. You will have much business to transact in that city. You both will have much to give and also much to learn."

Chapter III

POWER

We parted from Bentell after the great rains had finally swirled deep into the valleys and reached up all the way to the mountain. We traveled on foot several weeks, following the river Yumna.

We left the harsh rocky hills and our lonesome trail and welcomed the great expanse of fields opening below us, with its promise of human habitation and abundance of food. Indeed, every so often, we veered off the trail a short distance to visit a few huts of tribal people, gathered around a communal well. We were always well received, and though we could not communicate in their dialects, we were glad for the shared silence with others in the quiet evenings. The huts resembled each other and those of other parts of the country, with thatched roofs and stick walls, packed with mud and dried cow dung. The floors too were of stamped-down earth, swept each day, then washed with a mixture of water and cow dung. Often we met young girls on their way to the river bank. They carried empty baskets that they used to gather heavy silt which would help build a new hut or repair an old one. Early in the morning, the same girls would gather and kneed cow dung cakes from the surrounding fields and set them in piles outside their mothers' huts for the day's cooking.

Once we were overtaken by a group of people traveling in a brightly painted covered wagon drawn by a strong and docile bullock. They looked different from the people we had met in the fields; they were of darker complexion, and they wore brightly colored clothes in many layers. Their wagon had many mystical signs painted on it, and again, their language was different, incomprehensible to us.

Most of the women carried huge baskets on their heads, and on their backs, young children were slung in intricately woven and fringed shawls. Two of the older women had hennaed hair, hanging in many plaits, some with bits of strings and ribbons. They approached us and started walking on either side of us asking questions we could not comprehend.

One of the women gently took Essa's hands into hers, causing him to stop and turn toward her. Gentle trusting Essa relaxed his hands, opened into hers, and smiled. The old woman gazed into Essa's palms and with a startled look immediately dropped to her knees. She exclaimed a few words to her companion and now both were at our feet, kissing the low borders of our traveling robes. Gently, Essa pulled them up, and putting his hands over their foreheads, uttered a prayer over them, then waved them on their way.

The other travelers had stopped a little distance away to watch the scene in silence. Now the two women bowed deeply to Essa and me, and rejoined their wagon, where they immediately engaged in a hushed and excited conversation with their companions.

Eventually, we came to a village set by the river bank and obtained a boat that would take us down river to the confluence of the Yumna and the Ganges, at a place named Prayag. Two boatmen agreed to take us to Prayag, as they were going there themselves for an important religious gathering. So we settled with our provisions for a new life on the deep blue waters of the Yumna.

Early each morning, while our two boatmen were still asleep and the boat still aground in the dark silt of one or the other bank, Essa and I would sit in meditation. The mist over the river gradually lifted, and the sun shimmered on the gold-leaf of the landscape.

All day, the men took turns poling us along the river, Essa and I often insisting on sharing with the labor. In many areas, the river was lined with high cliffs, and holy men were known to live there in caves. We often peered into the shadows for a sight of them.

In many places we saw fishermen, pulling back on their nets, standing knee-deep in the mud and often quite naked except for more lengths of net wrapped around their head. Once, after a bend in the river, Essa pointed out to me some white shapes, glinting in the fiery midday sun, but as we drifted slowly closer, we discovered them to be a row of sun-bleached human skulls on a particularly bleak stretch of land.

The days passed on, similarly tranquil, and we were often content to watch the ever-present birds. Migrating geese in geometric formations moved to the northerly ranges. Ducks and egrets stayed at the water's edge. There were also terns, swallows, and many others we did not know by name.

The nights were less peaceful. Many strange noises were carried great distances on the northern winds of the chill night. Fish splashed, cranes beat their wings violently, jackals screamed on some deserted bank, and mud cliffs crumbled and rumbled down like thunder. Often I could not sleep but spent most of the night huddled, my legs drawn up into my robe. I felt miserable when dawn came, but I could scarcely complain to Essa. He always replied that sleep was unimportant when we had so few days to learn all that the river could teach us. Indeed he often sat through the night as well, in peaceful meditation, while I shivered and grew more and more tired.

Our progress was slow on the river but eventually we came to where the Yumna, the Ganges, and the Saraswati meet. One moment we were slicing the deep blue waters of the Yumna with our bamboo poles, and the next moment the water was universally ochre brown. The Ganges had completely swallowed the Yumna. There we encountered other boats like ours, with their bamboo canopies. Everywhere near the banks, people of all ages bathed in the holy waters of the Ganges.

Most of the people had erected small shelters for themselves on the ground between the two rivers for the duration of the religious festival. Everyday more people arrived on foot, their meager provisions in baskets and bundles on their heads.

We chose to remain on the other bank, away from the crowd. Here again, a high cliff dominated the water and was home to several saddhus who had dug themselves small caves high above the water's edge, accessible by some rough crumbling steps.

We arrived in the late afternoon and parted from our two companions. Soon we were readying ourselves for evening meditation, when a saddhu came and asked to join us. Later he explained to us that this spot, the confluence of the two rivers was the holiest spot on earth. One bathing here could not only be cured of diseases but be washed of all earthly sins as well. Certain times were particularly auspicious, and the many people gathered at this time were waiting for the very propitious partial solar eclipse that would greatly increase the power of the river.

The saddhu got up and went to bathe in the yellow froth himself, but we remained seated and meditated till the dark night overtook all around us.

In the morning, the saddhu approached us again and said, "Hurry and bathe. One never knows how much time one has left. This I have learned in many years of total renunciation, watching the two great holy rivers meet and flow by."

But Essa seemed unhurried. "Yes, we will bathe in the holy Ganges," he calmly replied. "But how can one cleanse the heart by washing the body? One should take time to reach the Father who dwells in the heart. Still we will bathe and then depart." And so we did.

Our two boatmen had come back for us the following afternoon, and again we set out on the river. The Ganges was more difficult to navigate, with its whirling eddies and undercurrents. We were very grateful for the boatmen's skill and strength. The banks on either side also became more foreboding, with dark dense jungle, and many crocodiles camouflaged in the mud, lying still in the hot sun. Everywhere, the abundant animal life kept us enthralled, with kingfishers, parrots, mynahs, hoopas, crows, and once in a while, even the wild antics of a tribe of gibbons swinging from tree to tree.

As we approached the city of Benares, the jungle receded once more, and we came upon brilliant green rice paddies gently swaying in the hot breeze. Here, too, we saw other boats like ours on their way to Benares, some rigged in pairs with a square sail tied between the two.

We arrived in Benares early in the morning, after another convolution of the Ganges. The mist rose from the waters, revealing hundreds of spires, temples, and ashrams roofs and buildings hanging over one side of the river. The sky was filled with pigeons and colorful paper kites, and everywhere the ghats or stone steps that line the river were already full, with men, women, and children waiting to bathe or drying themselves in the first sunrays.

Our companions pointed out to us the first ghat, where Shiva's wife was believed to have dropped her sword. They insisted that we stop to bathe our sins away before entering the holy city proper. They pointed out other ghats, one in Parvati's honor, one dedicated to Vishnu, one where four sacred and invisible rivers merge with the Ganges, and many lesser known ghats for the burning of the dead.

The rest of the city was a colorful maze of small streets and alleys, climbing up and away from the river and ending abruptly at some point in a mass of rubble. Between all the temples and shrines, hundreds of little shops and street vendors catered to the pilgrims and worshippers. Some sold the brilliant powders and sandalwood paste needed for the tilak spot on the third eye, rough clay saucers or more expensive little brass pots for oil lamps. Others sold images and effigies of the myriad of gods, goddesses, and other deities; silk scarves in gold, vermillion, and scarlet; bangles; jewelry; and precious stones. Everywhere, women sat stringing flowers into garlands. They were made with roses, the chiseled white champa, crimson hibiscus reserved for the goddess Kali, and the ever-present, ever-brilliant marigolds.

Then there were the less appealing sights of starving dogs and vultures turning incessantly around the funeral pyres on the cremation ghats. And there were amusing sights like the sacred cows disrupting traffic along the narrow streets, sometimes upsetting a vendor's stall and being immediately rewarded with a new garland of flowers around the neck. The incessant activity and the great religious reverence of the people lifted our spirits and increased our energy.

Following Bentell's instructions, Essa and I found suitable living quarters and prepared to settle in this city. We did not know what the third level of teaching would be, but we were happy to have arrived after our adventures on the holy river.

We settled into a small gray stone house on elevated ground several blocks from the Ganges river. The floor was bare ground and there was no furniture, but our needs were few. We each obtained a straw mat, and our robes served well as blankets. The air vibrated to the chimes of hundreds of temple bells, and everyday seemed to host a religious festival with great colorful processions to one temple or another. Occasionally, I asked Essa about the manuscript concerning the unusual Essene conception, but he consistently refused to discuss it and quickly changed the subject.

Here our life could be easy, pleasant, and satisfying. Every day, fruit and freshly cooked vegetables and rice appeared in our doorway, provided by Essa's friends. And everyday Essa would bring more friends to our small dwelling. As soon as all sat cross-legged on the bare floor, he would distribute banana leaves and share of our food equally with all.

Every morning, many holy men and revered Brahmins, at their chosen spots on one ghat or another, held readings of the Vedas to those who wished to attend. On many mornings, Essa could be found there, cross-legged and attentive as any other student. However, the knotted cords of the Brahmin revealed to others Essa's rank, and he often expounded on difficult passages. Essa displayed a sound grasp of religious problems and an intuitive balancing of analytical thought and mystical wisdom.

There came a day when Essa had his own particular spot on the ghats, and a group of people eagerly awaited his words. After sitting in silent meditation with his followers, in order to clear his mind and tune into his inner wisdom, Essa began: "Always remember to acknowledge the presence of our Father within you. He will always be there with you. He will never leave nor forsake you.

"When you have awareness of His presence, nothing else has real power over you. Mere temporal power is not real power except when we accept it as power. It need not control you. Spiritual power is the only true power. Acknowledge this with all your heart and this truth will set you free."

Essa continued: "What is your life worth if you spend all your time seeking power and money? You actually pay for these things with your life. It's no small sum. Your life is the most expensive price you can pay. Don't pay it. Save yourself this very moment. The kingdom of my Father is always at hand. It's here now.

"As you go about your daily affairs, remember to be conscious of the presence of the Father within you. Always remember that what you have accomplished is not nearly as important as how conscious you have been."

The people heard what Essa said, but did not understand everything. Yet they knew there was truth in these simple words. Often they left in small groups to discuss further his teachings and the man they knew so little about. Some said his wisdom was equal to that of the ancient sages. Others said he was illogical and many of his teachings were tainted with errors.

A couple of months passed and Essa's followers grew in numbers. Essa spoke openly and easily. Soon there were perhaps as many as a hundred young Brahmins who had heard what Essa preached and understood some of the truths that he meant to transmit.

Yet for all the worshipping of gods, goddesses, idols, and deities, for all the rituals and offerings and sacrifices, for all the genuine reverence of the sacredness of life around us, there was also an emptiness, a meaninglessness to the endless duties to the gods. It became a cause of dissatisfaction to Essa and myself.

Another and more serious problem soon became evident and centered around Essa's belief in the equality of men. This was in sharp contradiction to the caste system so firmly established in this part of India, which for thousands of years has separated people into different social groups.

Our small dwelling had remained open at all times to those who wished to come and partake of food with us or simply to meditate. And so we had an endless stream of visitors in white or orange dhotis.

One day, Essa came upon our gypsies of the colorful covered wagon—for gypsies they were—and they brought us a rich condiment of spiced mangoes, and gave each of us a delicate garland of the mango leaves, which the women had woven. We invited them in, but when the young Brahmins saw the gypsies sit with us and prepare to share our food, they refused to stay.

For a moment Essa was too stunned to speak. Then he slowly remembered other events he had chosen so far to ignore: the wretched individuals who seemed to come out only at night and compete with the wild dogs over piles of refuse; the poor multitudes who were chased or shoved out of the way of a rich rajah who ceremoniously approached town on a brilliantly decorated elephant, followed by a retinue of richly caparisoned ponies and caged leopards; the many faces suddenly averted, the avoided looks.

Now Essa wanted to know more about the cause for these separations among the people, and I did not hide my own disdain for the rigid and unjust system. I told Essa the facts of this system, the strict taboos against marrying or even eating with those of another caste, the elaborate duties and restrictions that dictate the life of the individual from the very moment of birth. I spoke with emotion in my voice, but tried to state the facts clearly.

"Ideally, the groupings of people in castes, which determine their rank and occupation, as well as the way they dress, eat, or worship, is meant to reproduce the perfectly harmonious world as it existed at the moment of creation. Each man, woman, or child, like each plant, river, mountain, bird, or beast, living at the proper place and in righteousness, should reflect the perfection of divine order. To deny one's place in the established order of society is not only to disrupt old and venerated traditions, but also to defy the Laws of the Universe. Lengthy codes have been established to identify and regulate the function of the four castes of people since the beginning of time.

"The highest caste, of course, is that of the Brahmins, who possess the holy knowledge and perform the rituals of the gods. The custodians of sacred Hindu scriptures and practices, they are all powerful and treated as well as divinities. You and I, Essa, because of our knowledge and aspirations, have been given honorary positions in this first caste. Ours is a most unusual situation and great privilege. For ages young men have had no other choice but to follow in their father's footsteps, and it is very likely that the two boatmen who so graciously brought us down here came from a family of boatmen who have poled up and down the Ganges as far back as anyone can remember.

"The next highest caste is that of the Kahatriya, the kings and warriors. They hold physical power, which augments the spiritual power of the priests. They rule under the direction and guidance of the priests. They are sworn to protect the priests and all the rules of society.

"The third caste is that of Vaishyas, the merchants, who run businesses, and the skilled craftsmen, who create all manner of products. This class also includes farmers, who constitute the largest group. Their work is often hard, and they lead a spartan existence. They do, however, often own their property and land. Also, they are almost never without food or the other real essentials of life.

"The fourth and last class are the Shudras. This lowest caste is comprised of the servants of others and has no rights.

"Each caste is strictly graded and segregated from the others. While the Brahmins teach and study, the Kahatriyas protect the land and study under the Brahmins. The Vaishyas provide the essential necessities of life for everyone through their crafts, agriculture, and animal husbandry, but may also study under the Brahmins. Only the Shudras, who serve the three higher castes, are not allowed to study the scriptures at all. In fact, a Shudra having accidentally heard part of the Vedas might be punished with molten lead poured into his ears.

"And then there are the untouchables. Outcasts of the system, they are considered unclean. Theirs is a terrible lot and they often have to do without the basic needs of life. They own nothing and work very hard in perpetual servitude. They toil at the most menial and degrading jobs. They receive no respect from the other castes and, in fact, are considered less than human. Whereas the upper three castes are ceremonially reborn into the caste and are known as 'twice-born,' neither the Shudras nor the untouchables can be reborn or permitted to enter the temples. They are not allowed to look into the faces of priests. A priest will immediately wash himself if he is accidentally touched by an untouchable or a low caste."

Essa had been patiently attentive to my speech, but when he fully realized that the lowest caste and the untouchables were not allowed to hear the religious readings, he became furious. Actually, he shook with rage, his eyes alive with angry determination. This was a side of Essa that I had not yet encountered. On the spot, he resolved to do something about righting this injustice.

It was then that Essa began his religious teachings in earnest. Essa saw a wrong he needed to make right. He wanted to teach anyone who wished to learn, regardless of which caste they came from. Soon the rumor of Essa's terrible ideas spread throughout the city.

When he went to the public bazaars, where food and merchandise were exchanged, he would talk to the people.

Essa preached: "Do not believe yourself first in all things. Know that he who is last is really first. Know that, in my Father's eyes, all men regardless of caste, are equal.

"I say to you that my Father's world is absolutely perfect in every way; yet there are poor and there are weak. I say you must help the poor and assist the weak. It sounds like a contradiction to attempt to change a world that is perfect, but it is the way of wisdom.

"Harm no one. Do not covet what you do not have. Do not become attached to what you do have," continued Essa.

Now Essa could be found in the most miserable huts scattered outside the city, laying neem leaves around the bed of a sick child or gently bathing a dying old one. Often the child would get well within a few hours of Essa's praying and loving touch. The old ones died in peace, the torment of their dreadful diseases suddenly and miraculously appeased.

As the knowledge of Essa's compassion and healings spread, furtive shapes started appearing at our door, often under cover of night, to ask Essa to help a loved one. Often he refused, gently explaining that he did not hold such power, but his refusal only brought on vehement beggings and gifts that these people could scarcely afford. Even then Essa was not quick to help.

First he would talk to them. "Blessed are the sorrowful, for they shall find consolation. Blessed are the hungry, for they shall be fed. Blessed are the sick, for they shall be made whole."

Next, he would ask if they truly believed that he could heal them. He would listen intently while they answered. Only then, if they really believed, would he work toward their cure.

He was careful not to take personal credit for his healings. Essa said: "I by myself can give only human comfort. Together, we will bring forth my Father to guide us through the problem. Miracles can happen only through his spirit."

Along with the healings, he taught the truths that he knew. He taught of the equality of all men regardless of their caste. He said his Father established no differences between his children and loved them all as equal brothers. Essa's words were in absolute conflict with the established viewpoint.

Even more dramatic were the changes occurring in the people's relationships with Essa. The young students who had been so delighted in his company, shunned him in the streets and plotted in small groups to inform the ruling Brahmins. On the other hand, some of the poorest people who had spent their whole life as down castes and then had been blessed with Essa's healing touch, turned toward him openly and bowed deeply in namascar, undaunted by the cruel punishment they were risking. Others fled in fear of the Brahmins' anger. Some said he was a king from some distant land. Some, however, said he was a colossal fool and a troublemaker. I started to become concerned over the political nature of Essa's sermons.

"Essa," I cautioned, "it is not good to mix your spiritual work with politics. The rulers of this land hear about everything of importance that is happening. When you preach against their system of castes, you challenge their power.

"The land is beautiful, the temples are beautiful and the people are beautiful," replied Essa, "but the truth is more precious than beauty. If we hide from the truth, our life will lose its meaning.

"But Essa," I continued, trying a new tack, "we must obey the laws and customs of the people we live with."

"I do respect the laws," said Essa. "However, it sometimes occurs that the laws and customs of a people are in conflict with higher laws. It's then that we must choose between the two laws.

"I cannot withhold my love for any man. I love the lowest as well as the highest. I cannot do other than speak of the brotherhood of mankind."

Essa seemed to have strength and fearlessness from sources unknown to me. I could not argue with him because in my heart I knew it was so. The truth and grace of Essa couldn't be denied. Still, the Brahman priests were the masters of this land. I knew that they would feel threatened and would possibly react dangerously.

During the next few weeks, Essa continued stubbornly to attack the caste system. His speeches were eloquent, and he persuaded many others to denounce this evil system. The numbers of people he had blessed grew rapidly, and news of his complaint spread throughout the city. Essa still did not perceive the dangers. He was absorbed in his own thoughts and work, in his healings, and in his goal of finding the hidden meaning of life. My intuition about the dangers of Essa's agitation against the caste system proved correct.

The priests' anger was very real and was fueled repeatedly with Essa's speeches. They were aware of the disquieting reaction of those who listened to Essa's words.

At first the priests hoped the situation would quickly return to normal. But Essa continued his attacks on the caste system. Essa now spoke daily of the equality of all men. Word spread to nearby villages, and the number of the poor and afflicted ones who sought Essa as their personal saviour swelled every day. And to all, he taught that no man can serve two masters and that the power of the rulers was nothing compared to the powers of the father.

The rising discontentment caused by Essa's new speeches among the priests knew no bounds. The need among the Brahmin priests and rulers to extract vengeance on Essa intensified. Their scriptures taught that anyone who spoke out against the priests should have boiling oil poured in his mouth and ears. The priests were very powerful rulers, and their power was soon to be focused on Essa.

I also was not without some friends. One of these kindred spirits brought me word about the latest slander and accusations. My friend said the priests were in the process of choosing an assassin to kill Essa. The rulers feared his growing popularity. Therefore, they decided not to kill him themselves. Instead, their plan was to have some local criminals do their work.

Essa did not fear death. But for him to continue ignoring the warnings would mean his suicide. I immediately found Essa and relayed to him the imminent danger to his person.

But Essa replied: "We all share in the responsibility for the events of our lives. The caste system is unjust, so I must be about my work and change it. I have no time to worry about the rumors you heard. We have been instructed by Bentell to stay here and do our work."

So there it was. Essa was unwilling to listen to my report. Normally, I would have deferred to his judgment. But in this case, the possible consequences were dire. I recalled Bentell's warning of strange and dangerous things happening and of threats to our very lives. Besides, Bentell had instructed me to assist Essa in his work, and keeping him alive would be one big assistance. I knew that not even the formidable power of Essa would hold up to that of the Brahmin priests.

"Listen," I shouted with passion, "this is no rumor!" Essa looked startled, since he had never before heard me shout so forcefully. I spoke quickly now that I had Essa's attention. "Please do me the respect of at least sitting silently with me and opening our minds in meditation. Let us bring our spirit to bear on the situation. Then the truth will surely be shown to us."

Essa knew that he could not refuse such a request. We sat together and meditated as Bentell had taught. Soon we were just watching the fleeting thoughts of our minds. In a state of detachment to these still occurring thoughts, we just looked. It was as if our whole existence were just a giant play, with us as the starring actors. We just watched. The play became a wheel. Our thoughts slowed down with this wheel. We stilled ourselves and centered our energy. As we quieted down, we reconnected to the presence of the Infinite Spirit. Our energies became powerfully centered, and the desires of the world could no longer hypnotize us. A grin began to form on Essa's face. It grew into a smile as he quickly came to see the truth of our situation.

Essa stood and hugged me warmly. "Thank you for being so determined," he said. "I see that our lives are endangered, and I struggled without awareness in a power conflict with the political system. I appreciate your wisdom in recommending that we leave the city of Benares immediately. I can see that the time of my usefulness in Benares is over."

Saying few farewells and taking precious little provisions, we departed. It was late in the day, but still bright outside. We walked quickly past women squatting, cooking their evening meals, and the aroma of spices filled the air, reminding me of my hunger.

We traveled only a few minutes when we saw many people walking in our direction. We hid behind an old crumbling temple, already half submerged in the Ganges, and watched. We were relieved to find it was a funeral procession on its way to a cremation ghat. Among the mourners were many priests, but they did not see us, so we continued out of town. We walked and walked, all night and most of the next day. Only when there was a safe distance between us and Benares did we stop to rest.

The following morning we continued our flight. With a deep heaviness in our hearts, we walked onward. One day followed another until, in a few weeks, we finally found ourselves back at the monastery in the loving presence of Bentell. Bentell gave us a blissful smile, suggestive of that of a parent awaiting a child's simplistic questions. Essa still somewhat attached to his good intentions and righteousness, felt our adventures in Benares had ended in failure.

"Bentell! I wanted so much to teach love and equality, but I stirred up so much hatred that I had to flee like a coward. Why send me to find work that I must then leave unfinished? Why show me injustice that I cannot right? Please share your wisdom with me.

"It's not what happens that determines if you are a success or failure. Don't think of success in the worldly manner. Name and fame are great potential pitfalls for a spiritual man. It doesn't matter what happens in your life. It's what you do with these life experiences that really matters. If you use them to grow, if you use them to complete the temporal portion of your humanism, then you are a success. Then you can go on to the next and higher level of experiences.

"But I was forced to flee the town," objected Essa. "What can I learn from such a negative experience?"

A smile played about Bentell's old face as he answered. "From your higher knowing, you were aware that the caste system was inequitable. Still, your spiritual power should not be used to change temporal power. Temporal power is that of false worldly concepts. They are false powers built by our minds.

"You became caught up in temporal powers to fight the battles between good and evil. Temporal power need not be power. When the power of the spirit is realized, then there is no other power. Then temporal power is no longer power.

"Instead of fighting with temporal power, you could have taught the people of Benares that they do not live by bread alone. You could have taught them to open their consciousness to the spiritual world. If they become conscious, the truths that were always within could then be released.

"All men already know everything that can be known about truth and justice. But usually they forget. They forget the truth and become obsessed with the struggle of one temporal power battling another temporal power.

"So speak to the spiritual reality of man and not to the illusions of temporal power. Then the spiritual forces will multiply, and the system of castes will change by itself. Feed them of your spirit and not of your body. Show them your stillness in the midst of the illusory storm. Give them of your hidden manna and they shall never want."

We dwelt with Bentell for many months. Everyday we meditated many hours and studied the ancient sages. I felt that I was experiencing great inner growth, that the false part of my personality was slowly and inexorably being shed like the cobra's skin, and that I communed more fully with my true inner self.

I was extremely happy as I learned and lived in the peaceful aura of my beloved master.

Chapter IV

AWARENESS

I never quite got used to the way Bentell suddenly appeared in our room. There was something uncanny about the way he came in. I never actually saw him enter. On one hand, it was exciting to see Bentell materialize and dematerialize at will. On the other hand, his appearances often annoyed me because he arrived when I least expected him.

Some of Bentell's students believed he could walk through walls. They talked of his being one with all existence. They said since he was not separate from anything, including walls, he could walk through them with ease. Indeed it was even said he had walked on water.

I once asked Bentell if it was true that he was able to walk through walls. His reply was that all things imagined are possible. He said his mind built no barriers to being able to do anything. Therefore, nothing was impossible.

Bentell is said to be one of the Saptha Rismis, a small group of enlightened masters who wander around the world. They help people to realize their spiritual enlightenment, appearing and disappearing as they like.

Today, Bentell materialized again. I looked up and there he was. He quietly stood in front of me with a very serious expression on his usually joyful face. I immediately became quite concerned. "My son," he began, "I have just received some urgent news that must be reported to you. Your uncle has just left his body.

"You mean he died?" I asked with a choked voice.

Bentell shook his head. "It is just a passing on that has mistakenly been called death. Still, you must travel home and be with your two brothers. You and Essa will pack some provisions and leave first thing tomorrow."

My uncle had been more than another relative to me. He had always been the family patriarch, the acting head of my family. His death would be a major crisis for all. I could see the wisdom in being with my brothers during this upheaval, but why take Essa along? There was no immediate answer, but I knew Bentell had his reasons.

Bentell continued: "It usually happens that you think what you are doing is the most important thing in the world. You give tremendous significance to even simple little acts. Then you get caught up in these acts. These acts tend to grow and become all-encompassing events. They increase in importance and soon your awareness is dominated by these dramatic fantasies. These in turn become so convincing that you believe this is the reality of your life.

"On occasion, you expand your awareness and remember that these personal events are not all that important. But usually you forget. You believe all your little acts are of tremendous importance."

Bentell gracefully gestured with his slender elegant hands. "Deep down in your inner core, you know there is nothing more important than anything else. After a certain amount of time, no one will remember what you did anyway. All the causes you worked and fought for will soon be forgotten. The monuments you build to yourself will eventually crumble. Even the great pyramids will last for but a flicker of eternity's flame. They will eventually return to the dust from which they came. Remember, all of the universe as we know it, from the day of its creation until its very last day is contained in the wink of Shiva's eye.

"So what you do is not really important, only how you do it. Just choose any act and do it. Know that it doesn't matter and yet do it as if it really mattered. This may sound like a contradiction but it is not. Perform your acts with total awareness. Then you will see the truth of them. Be aware each moment and do not live in your dreams of the future or of the past. It's perfectly all right sometimes to look at the future or past, but don't stare. There is an enormous power that comes from remaining aware in this present time. With this power will come a wisdom and understanding of the mysteries of life." Bentell paused, waiting.

Moments later, Essa walked into our room. Essa quickly and quietly bowed to the master, then sat down beside Bentell and me. Now Bentell continued speaking about awareness in terms of living each action and experience in a full and complete way so that we are able to appreciate its essence, while always remembering the insignificance of each action.

Bentell finished by saying, "Life is most meaningful when you experience the fullness that comes from the awareness of being totally connected to the universe. You then begin to see the truth that lies beyond your complex personal and really insignificant involvements.

"Go now and prepare for your journey."

We packed our clothing and ample provisions in woven satchels and retired for the night. We slept soundly until the birds awakened us at dawn. We ate hot grain cooked with milk, and got off to an early start, walking onward in the brisk coldness of the new morning.

We traveled on rugged pathways through the mountains, toward the headwaters of the Ganges River. Once in a while, we heard the clatter of hoofs, signaling a caravan and its small thick-set ponies, but we met no one. In the distance, loomed the outlines of the snow-covered summits. Among them was the legendary Kailas, where it is said Shiva hung his long matted hair from which the Ganges spilled slowly and evenly.

Before dawn we could only discern the immense sea of the clouds, as we meditated in the chill air. Then the sun rose and illuminated one mountaintop after another. I was shocked at the majesty, the beauty, as the peaks took on shades of pink, then crimson red, then gold. We were witnessing the flowering of the snows. When it was all over, we were ready to begin our day. Essa and I again were on the road, journeying toward our destiny.

However, this time there was no joyous anticipation. Instead, I dreaded having to interact with my brother Mangeshe. He had always been motivated by greed and often had tried to control others' lives. I was ashamed of his faults, and I could not help being critical of him.

What I disliked most was the prospect of introducing Mangeshe to Essa. I believed then that Essa would think less of me when he saw how my older brother treated me. Still, Bentell said that we were both to go, and I had learned long ago not to second-guess his instructions.

We ascended a high pass between two summits and rested beneath the shade of an ancient twisted cedar stubbornly rooted between the barren rocks. "Why won't you tell me about the Essene manuscript?" I abruptly asked Essa, prompted by my intuition. "Are you afraid?"

Essa's lip curled up to smile. "You're right. I don't know for sure if I was really conceived as the scroll describes. When I think about it, I feel pride and joy at my possible uniqueness, but above all, I feel fear. I don't know what is expected of me, or if I will be strong enough to accept my destiny."

This revelation made Essa seem much more human, and I felt much closer to him now. But now I also shared Essa's concern over future expectations of us.

Toward the end of the eighth day, we came to the village of Kotdwara, where I was born. We walked past an old shrine to the god Krishna, crumbling in disrepair and almost obliterated by dry weeds. Just ahead, several young children squatted on their haunches and giggled the way children do at the sight of strangers, all the time sucking on kumquats. We passed them, proceeded beyond a string of shanties with steep sloping roofs, and walked directly to Mangeshe's house.

The house was located in the more affluent section of the village. It was built of stones and shaded by tall silver birch trees. The house was large and pretentious. By worldly standards, Mangeshe was quite well off. His material wealth had obviously increased greatly since I last saw him.

Mangeshe greeted us in front of his elaborately carved door, and I gasped when I saw how old he looked. "My good Lamas, is that really you? You have really changed," he said. He appeared reserved and didn't reach out to kiss or even embrace me.

I smiled with difficulty as I greeted him. "Mangeshe, it's great to see you." Even as I spoke, I was horrified to realize that the first words out of my mouth were a lie.

I couldn't help staring at his pinched worried face. I forced myself to glance quickly in the direction of his wife, but in an instant my attention was brought back to him. "It's good seeing you, too," he replied. His voice was scratchy and even higher pitched than I had remembered.

"How many years has it been?" I asked in an attempt to overcome an awkward moment.

"About eight,

"No. I must have been away at least eleven years," I protested.

"It was no more than nine!"

There we were, already in an argument. I forced myself to act conciliatory and introduced Essa, while I grinned with a forced smile on my face. We entered Mangeshe's house. As I had foreseen, this meeting was already unpleasant. And I was reminded of the difficult times of my childhood. Mangeshe and his wife were married after I left, so this was the first time I had met her. She was striking in appearance, with raven hair, elegantly dressed in an elaborate silk sari with an embroidered border of gold and silver. She was adorned with massive jewelry of jade and ivory. She could be described as beautiful.

But there was a coldness about her that repelled me. I imagined the negative stories about me that Mangeshe had likely told her. He had probably told her about the simple-minded problems and conflicts I had created during my childhood years. Mangeshe loved to tell stories that put me in a bad light.

Mangeshe waved his short fat hands around and fussed over the stupidity of our recently deceased uncle. He was in a particularly bad mood. His long black hair was without luster and his shoulders were sprinkled with dandruff.

"Why should we have to kill three perfectly good oxen?" he asked. "The terms of your stupid uncle's inheritance are impossible." I listened to him fret for much longer than I thought possible. Mangeshe was even more of a greedy grouch than I had remembered.

"We will talk about this in much more detail tomorrow," said Mangeshe. He turned his attention toward Essa and asked, "What do you do for a living?

"I once was a builder of houses, but now I know that my only true vocation is to awaken to the truth of myself. For me, anything else is just an avoidance of reality."

Mangeshe shrugged his shoulders and turned away haughtily. To him Essa sounded simple-minded and he immediately wrote him off as a useless dreamer. An awkward silence was followed by Mangeshe's invitation. "When you arrived, we were just about to eat. You both must join us for dinner."

Mangeshe proceeded to show us the rest of the house. From the lavish entrance hall where we had stood and greeted his wife, we now entered the dining hall. A long low and exquisitely carved table stood in the middle, surrounded by thick embroidered silk cushions. The dining room opened onto a cool and shady courtyard. Several distinct apartments also opened onto the courtyard as well as the cooking quarters, which was a large square enclosure where Mangeshe's wife was now busy instructing a tired-looking young woman in a faded and frayed green sari. Mangeshe led us up stone steps to the upper apartment we would be using during our stay.

We returned to the dining room just as a servant brought our meal to the long wooden table. We began with hot puris served with tomato chutney, mango chutney, cucumber raitas, and side dishes of samosas, banana vedis, bharats in yogurt sauce, stuffed parathas, kofta balls, and curd pattis. The food was spiced just right for my taste, the white rice with cloves, the dahl with asafoetida and cumin and cinnamon, and I was pleasantly reminded of similar meals in my parents' house. Still my apprehension of Mangeshe's ill humor prevented me from freely enjoying the meal.

"Do you want tea?" Mangeshe asked as we finished the copious meal. We drank freshly brewed tea, heavily spiced with fennel and cardamon and cloves, and served in fine earthen bowls that I also remembered from my childhood.

I started to relax, while Mangeshe played with his empty bowl. Suddenly he gave me an almost mischievous look, then without warning, he started to laugh as though something extremely funny had suddenly struck him. Then he attacked me with his same old sick sense of humor.

Mangeshe spoke with his head turned away from me and toward his wife, as though they meant to share some secret about me.

"Lamas, do you remember when you were a boy how you wouldn't stop complaining about the awful racket that your pet cow made when he became sick?"

I knew what to expect next and felt like a penny waiting for change. I struggled to maintain my composure.

Mangeshe gave a soft chuckle under his breath and continued speaking, now to his wife, then to Essa. "When the cow half-kicked the fence down, Lamas was really upset. I told him there was a secret in caring for his cow that would keep it quiet. I said all he needed to do was to get a rope and tie one end to the cow's tail and the other end to a tree. Lamas completely fell for the story. He immediately went out and obtained a rope and tied his cow's tail to the tree."

Mangeshe paused to laugh again loudly and to encourage his audience for what was still to come. He continued with his little tale. "Well, that cow just didn't want his tail tied. He quickly turned on Lamas who was forced to run for his life. Lamas was so scared that he yelled louder than the cow. I got in a bit of trouble when our father heard the story, but it was so funny it was worth it."

Now Mangeshe's wife laughed loudly. I swallowed and looked at her with hostility. The perverse strength of her laugh continued to weaken my composure. I thought: "Here are two crude and insensitive people and they are well suited for each other. A cow could die before their very eyes and it would not touch them. They were probably too self-centered to even take notice of an animal's discomfort."

Essa threw me a quick glance, which said he had been listening closely and now had an inkling of what kind of man my brother really was. Essa looked at them with an amused air and a twinkle in his eye. He then said something that was strangely humorous, though I must admit that I did not understand it fully. "It is only he who is truly innocent, loving, and without sin who can gently tie a strong rope to a frightened cow's tail." Essa never raised his voice. He just let his sentence hang in the air, yet it immediately seemed infinitely funnier than Mangeshe's story.

Everyone at the table, as if under a trance, laughed heartily. That laughter, at the expense of none, was enough to lighten up the rest of the dinner and keep it from getting back into any argument. We finished the meal with small talk and were invited to stay the night in their guest room.

That night I awoke several times from a restless sleep, full of confusing dreams. I did not want to think about my brother, his problems with the inheritance of our uncle's oxen or anything to do with this family. But the more I banished them from my mind, the more I reflected upon them, and sleep refused to return. I raised my head, and in the moonlight I saw Essa sitting motionless in meditation. He turned to look at me, but didn't say a word and turned away again. His peaceful presence relaxed me, and I lay my head back down. I focused on the familiar sounds of crickets and particularly on the silence between the cricket's songs, the way Bentell had taught us to do, as that had always brought me tranquility. At last I slept deeply, without stirring.

In spite of the partial night's sleep, life at Mangeshe's house soon got back to its usual difficulties. Essa and I dressed and went to the dining area to find Mangeshe and his family already there.

Again, Mangeshe complained about our recently deceased uncle. "That old idiot is going to force us to kill three perfectly good oxen in order to receive our inheritance," fumed Mangeshe. He paced the room in agitation.

With a certain malicious pleasure, Mangeshe explained the details of our mutual problem. "Our uncle, before his death, awarded his oxen to us and to our younger brother. His allocation of his oxen was sensible. He gave one half of his total number of oxen to me, one third to our younger brother, and one ninth to you, Lamas." He looked down at me, and held a superior tilt to his chin.

"Unfortunately, at the time of his death there was not an even number of oxen. There were 41 oxen and that meant we would all end up with fractions of an oxen. For example, I would get 20 1/2. Since there is no such thing as half an oxen, one would have to be slaughtered in order for me to receive the full terms of the award. By simple math, our younger brother would receive 13 2/3 and and you, Lamas, would receive 4 3/5."

I quickly understood what upset Mangeshe. Some oxen would have to be killed in order for us three brothers to receive our just amounts. This meant that Mangeshe would get 20 live oxen and part of a dead ox. My younger brother would get 13 live oxen and part of a dead one. I would get four live ones and a portion of a dead ox. Unfortunately, that poorly executed will left us no choice. We had to divide it in this manner.

If one of us relinquished our fraction, another brother could have an extra live ox. Mangeshe said that he, as the oldest brother, should get the extra ox, and I should be happy. But I was unwilling to let Mangeshe get the best of me again. He must have had similar thoughts, since he also was uncompromising.

It was certainly a dilemma. I asked Essa for advice, hoping he could solve my problem for me. He also seemed to be without a concrete solution.

"Go behind the curtains of illusion, into the reality of the total," he said. This and other platitudes offered me little, except the hope that there was a solution I had not yet found.

I could have dealt with almost anyone except Mangeshe. I really had no great need for riches anyway. For someone else, I would have gladly given up my fraction of an oxen so that everyone else could have more. But Mangeshe had been taking advantage of me all my life. It was time that I stood up for my rights and stopped letting him have his way. I was, after all, an adult and should no longer be treated as a child.

Even if I had been tempted to let Mangeshe have his way, I also had to think of my younger brother. I had to set a good example in protecting my rights regardless of what Mangeshe said. I felt a yoke on my shoulders. Again I slept poorly that night.

"Ho ho ho, haw haw haw," laughed Essa. Every morning immediately upon awakening, he would follow Bentell's instructions and spend a few minutes in deep belly laugh, rolling around on the floor. By starting out each morning in this manner, Essa found it easier to keep from taking himself too seriously. Sometimes I laughed with Essa, but this morning I was unable to force myself to join him. It seemed to me this was indeed one of those rare exceptions when real problems exist.

Now Essa's laugh changed as though he had really discovered something of total hilarity. His laughter grew and grew until it took on the quality of a great cosmic laughter. It was a laughter that was one with the entire universe. The entire room seemed to shake with this cosmic laughter. It was irresistible. Essa's laughter became contagious, and I joined in not knowing why I laughed.

Now Essa was saying that in that moment, he received an illuminating flash that solved all my problems. His consciousness opened to the primal knowledge of the universe. He grinned at me as he contemplated the simplicity of the solution to my dilemma. Then he laughed some more, tears pouring down his cheeks.

"The solution, of course, is in keeping with Bentell's highest teachings." Essa beamed, then he continued: "If the estate of your deceased brother donated one ox to a poor needy family, it would be a good thing, wouldn't it? One who sustains his neighbor, sustains himself. It is strange how often donations result in more goods for both the receiver and the giver. Because by donating one ox from the forty-one, you and your brothers will each miraculously end up with one more ox than you would have had otherwise.

"After the donation of one, there will be a total of 40 oxen instead of 41. These 40 can be allocated so that your older brother gets 21. Your younger brother gets 14. And you will get five." That adds up to 40 so that all the oxen have been distributed.

"Now every brother wins. Each gets all live oxen. No oxen have to be killed. All this just from a generous donation of one ox. Letting go of your attachment to this one ox brings each of you an extra ox.

"Each brother gets more than he would have gotten had you tried to divide 41 oxen. Also, you would all have the good energies that come from contributing to another family."

I was astounded and asked, "Where did those extra oxen come from? I don't understand."

"At first, I didn't see them either," replied Essa. "Yet those extra oxen were always there. Because you had limited vision, you just didn't see them. You looked straight ahead like an ox yourself, with blinders on its eyes. You weren't aware of the alternate possibilities.

"It's exactly as you say," I exclaimed in amazement. A strange quiver went through my body, and I could not tell if it was from joy or relief. I now understood the solution and knew it would work. Once more I was filled with admiration and reverence for Essa. I felt deeply indebted to him and eagerly anticipated the time that I would be able to show my gratitude and allegiance.

I lost no time in telling the good news to my brother. Mangeshe stared at me with wide, fish-like eyes and a gaping mouth. He shook his head as though he had to think, and was unable to take it all in. Moments later, his eyes recovered their firmness. After all, my brother was a practical man. Twenty one oxen instead of 20 1/2 meant he was the winner and got an extra half. So Mangeshe agreed to this dispersion of the family wealth.

Essa saw that there was never really a problem. The only reason it appeared to be a problem was that we could not stand back and see the situation from a better vantage point. Instead, I had become involved in being right and proving Mangeshe wrong. We were in conflict, cut off from the unifying energies that normally guide the flow of our lives.

This teaching was obviously over. Confident that my younger brother's share was safeguarded, I felt no further need to remain in this unpleasant house. Essa and I packed our few belongings and began our journey back to Bentell. Yet on the trip back I was still troubled. I was confused and did not fully understand the meaning of this episode.

Essa obviously understood this teaching quickly. The heavy drama had easily become transparent to him. For me it was not that easy. I had been hypnotized by my previous relationship with Mangeshe, and I could no longer see my brother's true humanity through the dreams of my expectations. I had been unable to distance myself and obtain the necessary outlook.

Now in retrospect, I saw everything clearly. But I also knew that in the very immediate future I may get caught in yet another silly entanglement. How could I keep this from happening? It was a mystery to me.

We made excellent time on our walk back to Bentell's retreat. In fact, we returned faster than I thought possible. Leaving Bentell, we had traveled for a whole week, but coming back seemed to take only a few days.

Before I knew it, we were back at the peaceful retreat, sitting in the ever-reassuring presence of Bentell. In my most humble voice, I asked Bentell, "Can you help me to stay aware more often?"

Bentell looked attentively into my eyes, smiled slightly, nodded, but said not a word. Then he shut his eyes in meditation.

Sometime later, Bentell began to speak about the questions that bothered me. "When examining awareness, it's helpful to think about a tree. You can divide a tree into three separate systems. There is the root system, which is connected to the earth and draws up the necessary water and minerals. There is the branch system, which receives the energy from the sun and converts it to create the food and energy needed by the tree. And there is the trunk, which connects the two. The tree will thrive only if all three systems work together.

"Now think of yourself as a branch of that tree. Imagine that you are cut off from the tree. Think how it feels not to be attached. There is a sense of separation and of not being whole. If your branch is cut off from the source, it will bear no fruit, and it will wither and die. The branch by itself is nothing. This is how most people live their lives, feeling separate from humanity and the universe. Most people think of themselves as separate and dependent on no one. They are unaware of their true being. They become deluded and unhappy and seek a salvation in their struggle to acquire knowledge, money, health, power, and other temporary delusions. They will never find lasting happiness this way."

Bentell looked intently into my eyes, and I was transfixed. "The branch is fed only when it is connected to the tree, and thereby, connected to the root system and to the entire earth. When you become aware, you realize you are more than just a separate branch. You are more than a part; you are whole, you are complete.

"A branch needs the rest of the tree in order to get water and nutrients. If it remains separate from the tree, it cannot survive. It will quickly become diseased. It will wither and die.

"So it's the same with you. Your life will never work if you are separate from the source of your life. Every so often, stop your struggle and see the complete tree. Every day, remember your wholeness. Stop and be silent, and remember. Reconnect to the one.

"Remember you are not the branch, but the whole tree, and the roots are connected and part of the whole earth. You see, there are not really separate parts in a tree. That is only a concept. In fact, there is only one tree."

I looked lovingly at Bentell's hands while he spoke. They were slender, delicate, and almost translucent. They had the ethereal quality expected of those of an ascetic or a mystic.

"You ask how to remain aware in the face of constant illusions. One way is through daily meditation. When you meditate in stillness and quietness, you begin to hear the small voice within your center.

"Out of that inner silence, that small voice says you are not separate. You are whole. You become aware of the invisible flow of the infinite consciousness."

Essa gave me a friendly nod as Bentell continued. "The key is daily meditation. Don't be discouraged if you don't get immediate results. It's working. Even though you don't realize it, you will be quieting your mind and opening to the truth. Eventually you will find that you remain aware and are not mesmerized by the illusions of the world.

"When you remain aware, there cannot be real separation. Then there will always be an extra ox to give. And when you freely give to another's needs, your own supply will also increase.

"Relax and enjoy a well-deserved sleep, for your fifth teaching begins in the morning."

My hands dropped to my lap. I felt exhausted and drowsy. All thoughts slowed, disappeared, and my chin sank to my chest. I fell asleep.

Chapter V

UNIVERSAL LOVE

Essa and Bentell sat in stony silence, dwarfed by the great walls of the meditation hall encircling them. A wisp of sunlight darted through a narrow window facing the building's east side. As the day brightened, millions of dust particles danced in the shaft of light only to disappear again as the sun gradually dissolved into dusk. Still they sat, as if their day's meditation had passed in just moments.

Finally Bentell stirred, unfolded his legs, soothed his muscles with a gentle rub and slowly steadied himself upright. Now he paced slowly back and forth across the meditation hall until all the stiffness had left his body. At last he stopped in front of Essa. In a low voice, Bentell said, "Your next teaching will be universal love. Only in loving can you be fully realized. Merely being loved is insufficient. You must be the lover as well as the beloved. When love is allowed to flow through you, it cleanses and fulfills your true state of being.

"You, as a living breathing man of flesh cannot of yourself give or withhold love. Love comes from the Infinite Spirit and expresses itself through man. All love must flow first from the Spirit. Do not take credit for this love and do not expect any return from it."

Essa, overtaken by a desire to give love, said: "Master, may I wash your feet?"

As everywhere else in India, washing a spiritual master's feet was considered a great honor that brought one closer to God. Just touching the feet of such a master was believed to bring blessings. But Bentell rarely allowed his feet to be washed by anyone. Essa had never previously been granted this honor.

This time Bentell's reply was different. Bentell's smile radiated love. He nodded, then said, "Please wash my feet." Essa was equally surprised and pleased that Bentell chose this moment to extend the privilege. Was this a reward for his past progress?

Instantly recovering from being stunned at the honor, Essa answered softly, "It would give me great pleasure to be allowed to wash your feet."

Bentell sat on a large round cushion while Essa ran to the courtyard and filled a large red clay basin with water. Slowly and with great reverence, Essa touched Bentell's feet. A field of pure love was transmitted from Bentell's feet into Essa's hands and radiated throughout his being. Transfixed and completely captivated, Essa washed Bentell's feet. Essa's body was completely relaxed and slumped slightly forward while his eyes gazed straight ahead as if in a trance. He stroked Bentell's feet reverently. It was a gentle washing and Essa's face expressed a dream-like state of bliss.

In ignorance of the foot washing in progress, a monk suddenly entered Bentell's chamber with a message for him. The spell broken, Essa frowned. The monk caught Essa's critical look and realized he had interrupted a sacred procedure. "I beg your forgiveness, Master. I will come back later," he whispered apologetically.

But Bentell wouldn't let the monk leave so easily. He beckoned him closer and said in his most cheerful tone, "Your timing is most perfect. Stay and tell us what news you bring.

"The caravan with our semiannual supplies is approaching, so I came for Essa and Lamas to help unload it before nightfall. But since Essa is busy here we will manage without him.

"He will be happy to assist you," Bentell responded. "Go ahead, Essa, and we will finish this washing another time."

Essa's bliss was broken. Again he cast a reproachful look toward the monk. Essa stood, the contact with Bentell's love broken, and he felt himself slowly filling with hostility toward the monk. Yet he obediently followed instructions and prepared to assist in the unloading.

As they were crossing the courtyard, a sudden gust of wind came up causing Essa to blink. In a flash, his delusion of hostility had dissolved, seemingly carried away with the breeze, and he blossomed again into his normal loving self. He felt confused, unable to grasp what had just happened, but there was no doubt that he again felt love for this man as well as for all mankind. In the midst of all encompassing love, a door had been slammed shut, and now it was as if the wind had blown another open and a whole new perspective was in sight. Essa placed his hand on the monk's shoulder and together they walked out to meet the caravan.

Essa saw the small caravan approaching the monastery. It consisted of only four men and three horses, one of which was pulling an old rickety wagon. The horses were skinny, obviously malnourished and loaded down with far too much weight. In fact, nothing could be seen of a couple of them, except their four skinny legs and the very tip of their dark noses under the bales of cotton to be spun and the sacks of grains to be milled at the monastery.

A sour-looking little man with a horribly pock-marked face led the first two horses. He tied them to a wooden post in the courtyard, without even bothering to water them. He shouted orders to the other drivers in a harsh raspy voice, contradicting himself with each new yell, and quickly insulted everyone around him. The other drivers obviously feared this ugly demon and rushed about madly here and there, bowing to his orders. He showed no greater respect even for the monks.

Essa was appalled at the caravan leader's obvious mistreatment of others, animals and humans alike. He could not suppress the angry scowl knotting his brow together as more and more hatred of this despotic devil invaded him. Unable to sustain the sadness of the scene or the arrogance of the driver any longer, Essa turned away. Dancing shadows made by the last rays of sunshine were quickly climbing the upper eastern corner of the yard, and then they were no more. In an instant the light had shifted, dulling and brightening all at once, taking on a rose and golden glow. Essa felt a heavy veil lifting from his heart, and as he turned again to face the caravan, an expression of wonder spread over his face. There was not the slightest hint of hatred left in his eyes or on his brow or lips. He seemed bathed in love and, spurred by sheer joy as he ran forward to help unload, he could see that the ponies were really perfectly proportioned, their coats gleaming with good health and their eyes alert. Leading them in turn to the well-water was their leader, a small and gentle man of great compassion. Essa had to restrain himself lest he ran up to embrace the happy little man. The horses watered and at rest, everyone was soon at work unloading the small wagon.

Among the packages was a note addressed to Essa from his sister. Essa eagerly opened the note. "My dear brother," he read in her rigid schoolgirl handwriting. "I have come to India and am only a few hundred miles away. I fear climbing up the mountain, so would you travel down here and meet me? I have very important news to tell you."

Essa was delighted to hear from his sister after so many years' absence and immediately decided to go back down the mountain and speak with her. He informed Bentell of his decision, and they both agreed that Essa should leave the next morning with the small caravan.

The caravan carefully loaded a few scrolls that had been painstakingly copied by the monks of the monastery to trade for the unloaded provisions and departed, with Essa walking behind. The pace was very fast down the steep winding mountain road and they took no rest breaks.

For a while they had been following a deep gorge, the little narrow wagon almost wider than the path itself. They steadily descended until the path ended abruptly and they came to a suspended bridge built of strong ropes and bamboo slats. The river rushed far below the bridge, crashing into the rocks, and it was a difficult and slow business to steady the horses across. The men each held one firmly at the bit and encouraged it in a firm voice. Essa trailed behind, wondering how difficult the trip up to the monastery must have been, with the wagon and horses loaded heavily. He was growing full of admiration for these rough mountain traders and their animals. Now the murmur of the water below sang to his ears and he turned back to gaze upon the rocky mountainside they had just descended and a succession of small waterfalls a little way up river. Where the water crashed onto flat rocks, the slanted evening rays created rainbows in the spray, and the deep blue sky reflected in the pools to the sides of the deepest fall.

Essa stood entranced by the beauty of the spot, the sheer magnificence of unspoiled nature. He stood still on the bridge, his heart and thoughts uplifted, blissfully unaware of the caravan that had resumed its quick pace downhill.

The caravan was soon far ahead of Essa and out of sight. Now he had to hurry to catch up. The steep road took a sharp turn and then forked into two roads, one appearing to go back up the mountain, the other down. After a moment's hesitation, Essa took the downward road and started at a brisk pace. However after ten minutes, the path began to rise again, and soon Essa became concerned that he had chosen the wrong road. He was now completely separated from the caravan and unsure as to which way to proceed. He turned around and retraced his steps back to the fork, taking the other road, but now he knew he would not ever be able to catch up with the caravan. The sun sank low behind the mountains, and still there was no sign of the caravan. Essa walked on, concerned about being lost and alone in an unfamiliar region.

It was dark now, and a brisk breeze blew cold wet clouds into Essa's face. Ahead, he could barely see the outline of the wreck of a deserted shrine that stood broken down and roofless. The wind rattled a few loose stones and produced a strange quaking sound that sent shivers through his body.

Presently, strange shapes swept by, seemingly carried by the squalls of wind and moving too quickly to identify. Essa stood still, leaned forward, and braced himself against the force of the wind. The strange shapes came into focus more clearly. Essa saw faces, dark angry faces glaring at him.

Now the clouds lifted entirely, and the bright moon illuminated a mob of people surrounding Essa. He stood, unable to move, unable to understand where these people had come from. They could not have all hidden behind the old shrine. They made a menacing circle around him, a couple of vicious-looking dogs dangerously close to his calves. Some of them shouted and waved their fists at him, the dogs began to bark furiously, but no sound came to Essa's ears. He strained to see and to hear, frozen in panic, but the forms remained shapeless and dark, only the terrifying faces identifiable, and no sound reached him.

Still they gesticulated, coming closer, some brandishing sticks and long knives. Essa felt a slight movement behind him. He spun around just as an enormous black hand reached up for his throat.

Now he was running uphill, stumbling onto loose rocks, unable to look behind. The wind began to howl behind him, urging him to run faster and faster. Because of his fear and the altitude, he soon could hardly breathe at all and fell to the ground exhausted.

Underneath him the ground itself seemed to want to buckle up, heaving and groaning. Everything, the strange faces, the howling of the wind, the ground itself repulsed him, and he thought he might be losing his mind. He realized that he was completely surrounded and overpowered by evil forces. Essa raised his head to peer into the darkness for his pursuers when a large king cobra, at eye level and only a few feet away, shocked him to attention. Its lower body was coiled and its hooded head weaved back and forth in readiness for strike. Essa no longer had enough energy to rise from the ground and run, so he succumbed to defeat and surrendered. He stopped shaking and watched the undulating patterns on the cobra's neck, the smooth scales and the graceful curves. If he must die now, let him surrender to this perfect creature. Out of the corner of his eyes, he saw the dark shapes again, but he no longer feared them. He would meet with the cobra in a last acknowledgement of life and surrender to its deadly power. He yielded to all the repulsive and horrifying forms. Essa accepted them, surrendered himself to them, offered no resistance, and in an instant, the delusions ceased.

The wind stopped blowing and howling, the ground stood still under him and filled him with warmth, the cobra vanished, the moonlight enveloped him with softness, and universal love filled his heart and soul.

Essa sat up, crossed his legs, and quietly meditated on his strange situation. He sat silently and utterly empty for what seemed like hours; then he became aware of strange noises off in the distance and strained to identify them. He was overjoyed to realize that it was the caravan that had doubled back in search of him. The little caravan leader happily grinned as he spotted Essa. Essa ran toward the caravan and warmly embraced the driver. Essa felt happy and safe and, since it was dark, the caravan prepared to spend the night there on a stretch of gently sloping meadow.

"We were worried about you," said the caravan leader. "As soon as we missed you, we stopped and waited for you to join us. After a while I decided to turn the caravan around and search for you.

"I am thankful for my rescue. I believe that I became quite lost. Please allow me to wash your feet as a token of my gratitude," replied Essa. Essa filled a red clay basin with water and began the gentle washing of the caravan leader's feet.

Essa softly stroked the caravan leader's feet, and as he massaged them his mind began to drift, so that the mountains and caravan became cloud-like and soon disappeared completely. Essa suddenly realized that Bentell's feet, not those of the caravan driver, rested in the wash basin. Essa's confused and racing mind abruptly stopped, and it seemed as if all eternity suddenly existed at once.

Essa was no longer on the trail. The forest had really disappeared, and Essa saw the familiar surroundings of Bentell's meditation hall.

In deep awe, Essa gently rubbed Bentell's long slender feet. Slowly Essa's mind began to focus again on the moment. He realized that in truth he had always been rubbing Bentell's feet, and the caravan leader was an illusion. He had been deluded, and, in reality, he never had a sister and had never been lost on the mountain trails. With that discovery he reached a safe harbor. Warmth and light poured over him. His face showed no signs of his recent fright. On the contrary, he looked more serene and beautiful than ever.

After the washing, Bentell said to Essa, "I must congratulate you." Then there was a typically long period of silence. Today this sharing of the silence seemed even more stark compared to the turmoil Essa had just been through.

Finally Bentell continued, "Your quality of universal love is extremely strong, and it overcame the illusions projected toward you."

Essa interrupted Bentell. "Can you actually make me think what you want? Was everything a dream? Was my whole life a sham? Are you and Lamas and I just illusions without real substance?

"No, no. We are not a dream. We are real. Life does exist. There is only the one spirit, which creates all that we know as reality. But usually we forget; we project illusions onto reality so that this one appears to be many. It's every man's choice to either hate the perceived differences or to remember that we are all the universal one toward which there can be only universal love.

"But make the smallest distinction and the universal one is hopelessly divided into many. This division is but a mere shadow of reality that so beguiles the small self with never-ending change, that it is believed to be reality. The same woman can appear to different observers to be a wife, a mother, a daughter, a stranger, or even an enemy. They are all correct. They are all real; they are all one.

"You were caught up in many dark, bleak, and loveless little dramas, each was initially threatening and fearful, but your love transformed this illusion into peace and joy. You always were a man of love and there was no way you could become entangled in a situation without love. And your love set all things right. You quickly saw through all the unloving veils of illusion."

It was quiet and they sat still in a state of grace for a few moments. Then Bentell continued speaking, but now his voice seemed to come from everywhere.

"We all create our reality, minute by minute. Somewhere within us we all know that we really are the creators of our own unique universe. We can choose to see either beauty or ugliness. We hold within both the gates of heaven and the gates of hell. Most people, however, ignore this infinite power within them." Deeply moved, Essa sat motionless, dwelling on every word.

"So no longer ask about reality. Just know that your universal love makes any further teachings on this subject unnecessary. When a tree has an overabundance of energy it creates flowers. The tree takes this excess energy and creates a glorious beauty that eventually seeds and recreates itself. You, Essa, also flower with an excess of universal love, and it is indeed beautiful to behold."

Bentell closed his eyes for a few minutes. Suddenly his forehead was deeply furrowed as though some inner vision distressed him deeply. Then once more he riveted his penetrating eyes on Essa. "Soon you and Lamas will leave the monastery and receive your sixth teaching. But beware. Your very lives will depend on your total awareness and faith."

These last words were spoken without his former mildness.

Chapter VI

FAITH

During the last four months, Essa and I had been living near a very small village, high in the mountains of northern India. There, life had been peaceful and rewarding, and we had learned to no longer question small details, like why we were here or what might happen next. We did, however, concentrate on staying alert as we awaited our sixth teaching. We remembered Bentell's warning about remaining aware of possible dangers.

This morning the sun had broken faintly through the clouds, and a pale light had filtered into my room as I awakened. I had been dreaming about Essa and Mangeshe and that extra ox. For a moment, I believed myself still in my brother's house, maybe because the sunlight dancing surrealistically on the walls belied the cold outside. How typically obnoxious Mangeshe was, but he didn't beat me that time. A smile spread over my face. This was all far behind us now.

I walked out to a distant field to relieve myself and shivered in the morning cold. It was early autumn and multi-colored leaves floated down from the trees at the slightest breeze and laid a carpet beneath them. Today we would leave these high cold mountains and travel into the valley. There we would dwell and escape the extremes of the approaching winter.

I walked downhill to warm up near the morning cook fire. The fragrance of the burning pine wood mixed with the dampness of the morning dew, and smoke spiraled up into a grey dancing column. About thirty travelers had spent the night near this fire. They, too, were awake and now moved closer to the flames.

These travelers were all sick people, who had assembled here in the hope of being cured of all manner of disease. When Essa came to join us, they asked him for cures. Still Essa never volunteered to cure anyone of anything. But these wretched souls had traveled many days to ask for Essa's blessing in the hope of a miraculous healing. Some were rewarded with an audience with Essa, but their chances of being healed depended more on themselves than on Essa. Miraculously, many left with their hopes fully realized.

Essa often said he could not of himself actually dispense wisdom and cause the diseased to become pure and whole. He admitted that a wise teacher cannot give to another the temple of wisdom. All he could do was bring another to the threshold of the temple. Essa had many times stated that each man must eventually cross this threshold and realize his own understanding of wisdom and faith.

During these past four months, Essa had been more of a healer than a teacher. Each morning, he had spent some time healing those who gathered around the blazing fire. To those gathered around watching, Essa indeed appeared to be a healer endowed with miraculous gifts to cure the body of all manner of disease. But to those fortunate beings whom he ministered to, Essa was revealed as a healer of the body, mind, and soul. He was a healer of the whole person, integrating the three, and making them one.

Presently, Essa completed his morning meditations and breathing exercises; he dressed and stepped outside. Essa came down the hill, and the crowd around the fire spotted him. Immediately the poor wretched souls dropped their meager breakfasts, mostly pieces of day-old bread and leftover rice and yogurt, and they eagerly approached Essa, calling on him to begin their cure immediately. Today they were particularly anxious because they knew this would be Essa's last day in this village, and many had traveled from afar and had waited several days.

An emaciated disease-ridden man was brought to Essa on a stretcher by his weeping relatives. In a scratchy, almost inaudible voice, he whispered, "Please sir. Please, if you would only cure me, I would do anything. I am miserable and have not not been able to move since I broke my back in a fall three years ago."

Essa looked down at the man and said to him, "If you would learn just one thing today, learn faith. Nothing else is needed. If you have a physical affliction and are miserable, nothing else will work as well. If you have lost hope and meaning in your life, learn faith.

"Each of you who believes with all your heart will find yourself freed and made whole. You will realize your union with the One and be healed. Both the best and worst of you can be immediately relieved of your suffering through faith.

"It takes only a split second. What you think of as time is but a limited view of the possibilities available. In an instant, your faith can stop time. Your faith can merge past, present, and future into one. A healing that should take years can be done now in this very moment. In this indefinable instant of time, all eternity exists.

"Why wait for a cure to develop? Don't even wait until your next breath. This very moment, your faith will heal you. Your total trust and surrender to my Father will make you whole. Don't wait and hope. Simply surrender. Surrender completely to the love of our Father, and claim your wellness.

"I am talking about total surrender. Don't surrender to me as a person. I alone can do nothing. Surrender and have faith in my Father, who pervades the entire universe. Allow His love to illuminate, and make your dark sins vanish.

"You are already healed, but don't yet realize it. The choice of sickness or wellness is yours, and yours alone. Choose wellness and the pain is gone forever. Open your eyes and see that all is perfect. See that you are also perfect, and the power of my Father surges within you."

Essa leaned down, laid his hands upon the invalid, and said, "Be whole again." Immediately his afflictions were banished and he slowly started to rise from his stretcher, first with great difficulty, turning and twisting sideways, and pushing himself up with his skinny arms. Then he sat up on the edge of the stretcher for a little while, as if to muster all his energies. When at last he rose, his arms spread out toward the sky and his face awash with a glowing light, the crowd stood mesmerized by the poor man's efforts, and a murmur spread like a wave in view of the amazing miracle.

Essa spoke quietly now to a blind man. "You need not struggle. It is not you of yourself who can do anything. It is our Father who gives us life and health. Forgive yourself when you stumble and fall. Just trust and have faith in our Father. Stop singing your mournful songs of disease and listen to the harmony and love of the universe. If your distrust is the size of a small mustard seed, your faith is as nothing. Hold back no longer. Have total faith now!"

Essa stretched out his hands and laid them upon the blind man and he could see. The newly cured man said, "Thank you, oh, thank you, Lord Essa," falling to his knees and kissing fervently the edge of Essa's robe.

But Essa would take no personal credit. He responded, "Don't give credit to me. It is your very own faith in my Father that has made you whole again."

Essa's whole effort was in assisting these people to return to the Father. He wasn't talking about belief. On the contrary, belief in a dogma would not be enough. Belief is only an idea of the mind. Essa was talking about the faith that only comes from total and absolute knowing.

Essa again addressed the group. "If you lack faith you will perish, and the darkness will block out the light. But even then do not fear because again and again you have the opportunity to come in out of the darkness. But why wait? The next sunrise is already upon us. Wait no longer. Why wander in the darkness even another second?"

Yet I knew Essa's words mattered little. The deaf man was cured, but he had not been able to hear, so the magic lay not there. Some hung transfixed to Essa's eyes, receiving darshan through him. But the blind man, too, had been healed. It was a total transmission that defied my ability to describe. Essa once called it practicing the presence.

Essa spoke again to the crowd: "If you have faith and trust, no one can deceive you. On the contrary, it is your doubt that deceives you. When you have faith, you have eyes that can really see the light. You have ears that can really hear the word. No one can ever again convince you that it is dark, once you have seen this light. Your faith can move any mountain that hides the light. Belief is only a trick of the mind; go beyond belief. Go to total faith, and you will receive the inner grace.

"I know you cannot cure my disease," said a slightly built man with crippled legs. "But will you show me some small miracle? I want to experience it myself rather than just see others being cured."

As he spoke, he crept toward Essa in a crab-like fashion, pulling himself along with strong arms, his legs dragging pitifully behind him.

"Your question exposes your lack of faith," Essa replied. "The miracles of God began when the universe was created. They occur at each and every moment. If you do not see this, you are deprived of the most beautiful gift of life. That you are alive is in itself a miracle. Enough foolishness."

The cripple reached to touch Essa's feet, but he remained crippled. After healing only the truly faithful, Essa returned with me to our humble cabin.

Bentell had instructed us to leave this mountain village before the fierce winter cold set in and the mountain passes iced over. We were to make our winter home in the less brutal climate of the lower hills and valleys. These last four months had been the most rewarding and peaceful of my life. Positive energy renewed us daily from the majestic beauty of the snow-capped peaks, the array of colors reflected off of them as the sun rose and set, the vibration of light at dawn and dusk, the mist hanging in shimmering rose-gold layers, and the sheer power of the mountains.

The mountain people were hardened by the altitude and harsh climate, their faces deeply lined by the winds and sun, resembling the deep jagged lines of their beloved surroundings. But they were both happy and generous, free of suspicions and prejudices. Essa wanted to stay with them much longer, but there was no more time.

For the last few weeks, I had watched the frost settling in at dawn, and I had repeatedly told Essa that it was time to leave. Finally he agreed. Today we would begin our journey to our new winter home.

In spite of their simple living, each one had to bring us a parting gift. All who had been healed in the village had somehow arranged to procure a gift such as a white wool scarf, butter and yogurt, bread and other foods. Unable to refuse these offerings of the heart from such gentle people, we arranged for a couple of traveling packs to be slung over our shoulders.

The first leg of our travel would take us higher up into the mountain and across a narrow pass, which was already covered with snow. There, our guide and his yak would leave us. He walked barefoot all year round, pulling his beast behind him by a strong rope attached to a ring in its nose. He would continue climbing higher into the mountain range to deliver the butter and other goods packed on his animal, and we would walk down along the eastern route, which was steep but relatively short.

It is difficult now to relate this part of our journey because of the catastrophe that occurred. The lost opportunity to remain longer with Essa will always haunt me. Still, I will do my best to finish this telling.

Travel in these mountains was treacherous at best. Because of the recent rains, the trail was especially slippery and very hazardous. The day we bade farewell to our guide and his yak and started down the mountain was bleak and cloudy, and with winter approaching fast, the weather was bound to worsen. In a few more days, when the trail iced over completely, the steep ravines would become impassable.

Down and down with long measured but careful strides, we walked through this section of sparsely forested mountains until the weakening evening light and our inability to see in front of us forced us to stop and make camp for the night.

I will never forget the second day of our trip. I awoke chilled to the bone, stamped the cold out of my feet, devoured a piece of bread, and we resumed our trek down the mountain. Due to my inactivity of the last few months and the damp cold, I had developed a catching pain inside my right knee, but hoped it would heal. Instead it got worse and the pain did not let up. The pain caused me to feel slightly light-headed, and I had a foreboding of all the pain I would soon suffer.

The sky was darkening rapidly. Gusts of wind blew fitfully, and the roar of thunder crashed menacingly through the clouds. Rain and hail poured down on us intermittently, and made rivers out of the ruts in the path. Presently we were caught in a wild violent tempest. Soaking wet, bitterly cold, and seeking shelter, we climbed down a particularly steep trail, hardly able to discern a few feet in front of us. I wanted to be careful, but I also rushed along in the dark in my urgency to find a cave or a shelter of some kind where we might rest awhile. I became angry at the elements, groping and stumbling forward, I wasted my diminishing energies in battling nature instead of surrendering myself to the reality of the storm. I fought the elements, pushing steadily downhill, staying close to the edge to avoid the rushing stream, and stepped on a loose and wet stone. I felt my foot slipping, then the stone tilted slowly over the edge and I was falling. I clawed at the wind and rain and there was nothing to grasp. Then, in a flash of lightning, I saw Essa's face over me, and I heard myself screaming his name. He was trying to grab me but he was too late. A part of me was denying the whole event. It could not be happening, not to me, not now. As I hit and bounced off of a couple of rocks, jolts of pain shot through my back, my limbs, and my head. Still, I fell, and I was suspended in sheer terror.

Then in slow motion, I saw all that was happening. It was all part of a large wheel and the wheel spun around. All the previous events of my life fit perfectly in the scheme of things, and I was filled with love for all the actors and participants in all my past personal dramas. I relaxed some as I landed in a clump of thick bushes.

The pain in my back was overwhelming and caused me to sweat profusely. I shivered, and tried to look through the rain and my tears, but all seemed to fade away in a somber mist, which I imagined to be my continuing separation and death.

I must have temporarily lost consciousness, because the next thing I remember was Essa kneeling next to me. He was speaking softly. Very slowly his words began to take on meaning. I was shocked at the grief and horror on his face. Tears streamed from his eyes.

"Oh my Father," his voice rose. "Lamas is a good man. Bless him with your divine compassion. Heal him and make him whole."

As I became more lucid, his voice began to calm down and take on his usual gentle quality. I hoped that this meant he knew I would quickly recover. I gathered my strength and tried to focus more on what Essa was saying.

The fear and grief I originally perceived in Essa had now totally vanished. He was now pure positive energy. I began to feel lighter and less tightly bound to my hideous situation. I held onto his words, putting all my faith in his power to heal me as he had healed so many before.

Then from deep within a tremendous shock of pain rose up and invaded my senses, obliterating all other consciousness. I was horrified and powerless as I felt my strength drain away.

Still Essa was speaking: "There is the spiritual law, and there is also the material law. Your injuries are on the material level. It is as if your body was tied down with sturdy ropes. Know that the spiritual law is above the material law. The spirit cannot be tied down with any rope.

"Rise up now without fear. Realize that the spirit within is your true being. Open your heart wide unto the body of life. Have faith and trust in my Father, and He will make you whole. Lamas, rise!"

I held onto Essa's command with all my soul but my body shook with pain and cold. With all my heart I wanted to rise, yet the fear and the pain kept me paralyzed on the ground. I wanted to believe yet I was afraid that I was about to die. Less and less could I distinguish Essa's voice from the sounds of the hostile storm.

Essa. I thought of Essa. I had to get up and go to Essa but I knew that my body was broken and useless. A blinding white light engulfed me more and more, and I felt less conscious of the pain as if it affected another part of me that I could isolate and maintain at bay. I was still tied to images from the past rushing back and forth through my mind. My mother's smile, Essa offering a flower to the bandit, Mangeshe and his wife jeering at me, Bentell's beautiful face in meditation; all filled me equally with a quiet peaceful joy. I was thankful for all. Every moment had been perfect and now I understood that I, too, had been perfect. Every moment of my life had been a universe in itself, as in the blink of Shiva's eye, and I had been Shiva!

I wanted to tell Essa not to weep. I had witnessed so many miracles and I expected him to heal me too. "Rise up," Essa again commanded but my body was mangled and weak and did not move.

A magnetic power slowly left my body, tingling at my fingertips. The white light was all around me as well as through me now and I felt myself drifting up on it. Then I was the white light. Looking down, I could see my still body lying there before Essa.

I was dead.

Chapter VII

REALIZATION

I was vividly aware of the final acts of my life, and the departure of my physical body. Leaving my body felt like taking off a heavy and cumbersome winter coat. I experienced the rapture of release. My senses were all vivid and pleasant. Sounds became more harmonic, colors more intense. I felt lighter, freer, and very peaceful.

Death is not the end. It is simply a transition, from one reality of life to another. I wanted to tell Essa this, and to thank him for sharing his life with me, but he could not hear. Essa did not yet accept my reality of life and death. So for him, this was one of the darkest moment he had ever known. From the depths of his despair, he wept uncontrollably. Waves of nausea wrenched him. The cold reality of my death slowly and painfully overcame him; he could not divert his thoughts from the Lamas he knew, and he still thought I was the twisted lifeless body in front of him.

The more deeply Essa thought of the Lamas he knew, the more he trembled inwardly. Filled with doubts, tears poured from his eyes, tears that he hardly was aware of, yet he could hardly see. Doubt took place where faith had existed.

Essa started to blame himself: if only he had agreed with me to start the descent of the mountain earlier. If only he could have grabbed me quicker and had prevented me from falling. Why wasn't he walking in front, leading the descent? If only he had had more faith in his Father's presence. He thought his lack of faith had failed me and he had been unable to save me from death. He would not be able to summon the faith again to heal others.

The light left Essa's eyes. He stared straight ahead, but saw nothing. The storm had abated and the sun filtered tentatively through the clouds, but for Essa there was no blue sky or sunshine. Everything was dreary, dark, pointless, hopeless. Never had he been so alone. His guide, friend, and spiritual brother now lay dead. Essa knew that he had somehow failed me, his brother, and he would forever walk with only despair for a companion.

But the darkest hour gives birth to the new day. So it was with Essa. Essa forced himself to take care of my remains. He carefully laid my body under a small rocky overhang, straightening my wet hair and traveling garments as best he could. Then he wandered around the bushes in the ravine in order to gather branches and leaves to cover my body with. It was late afternoon and the crickets started their monotonous chanting. Essa remembered how we had practiced meditating on the rhythm of the crickets' song, then on the rhythm of the silent intervals in their music, as taught by Bentell. We had traveled together many times with the crickets' syncopated melody, and we had touched the universe. Essa remembered how I had started imitating the little insects and how good I had become at it. A smile spread over his face. Essa understood that wherever crickets sang, he would find me.

In denial of his illusions of the imperfections of life, he shook his head violently from side to side, then stopped still and spread his hands toward the sky. In humble veneration, he bowed low and touched the earth with his forehead. He called on the forces of the universe to bear witness to the spirit within him. The veil of illusion had lifted. He saw that death is part of life and fully realized that nothing in the visible world lasts forever.

Essa realized that my death meant simply that I was not here in physical form. He remembered that my true self still existed. Essa lowered his arms, straightened his back and heard the voice of the Father. The sweet sounds of birds and the cosmic hum of all existence returned to his ears. Essa now accepted, without resistance, the infinite reality, and all tears were wiped from his eyes.

A globe of fire slowly rose toward the sky and lighted his vision until everything was radiant. Essa was home.

The mystical tones of large temple bells vibrated throughout his body and opened his soul to God's love. He looked around him and saw the world again, as if for the first time. The sunlight illuminating the mountains had just been created, so had the mountains, trees, rocks, bushes, and fertile valleys in the distance. The greens and golds and yellows of the patchwork fields had never radiated so before, the blue of the sky had never held such depth. All was beautiful and vibrant.

My life force had ebbed out of my body and enriched all of creation. Essa stood at the center of God's creation. He blinked and when he opened his eyes, he saw that he was back at the monastery. But the monastery also was completely transformed. Almost everything was changed and Essa found few familiar landmarks.

Gradually a luminous form appeared. "Bentell," Essa whispered almost inaudibly.

Bentell looked different. His face was timeless, neither young nor old, and he smiled an absolutely beautiful smile. Some enchanting force emanated from him and surrounded him. Regal robes of silver and gold brocade replaced his normally humble clothing.

Essa neither advanced nor retreated, but began to turn his face away from Bentell. But no matter in what direction he turned, he still saw Bentell.

Essa fell down in awe at Bentell's feet. But Bentell motioned for him to rise and said: "I am your fellow servant. Do not worship me."

Dazed, Essa arose and asked, "What about Lamas? Why did he have to die? Was he also a dream?"

Bentell focused his kind clear eyes on Essa and spoke: "There is no death. There is only the belief in death. Life goes on and on in infinite form and infinite variety. His life never had a beginning and never will end. Lamas has gone to a new and freer experience."

Essa started to say something, but Bentell cut him off. "Be still and know the answers are all already within you. The path is not straight up. Often you fall and become entangled in the suffering of temporal life. That is just the way spiritual growth is. It may seem that you are back doing the same old things and thinking the same old thoughts that you always did. But something has changed. You can never go back to sleep completely, once you awaken. For each of us, the overall direction is toward the higher truth.

"There will still be shadows and darkness, but light will prevail. The sleeping being who is stirred will never again sleep so soundly.

"At your conception you were chosen for a special purpose. That is to remind your brothers of their connection with the Infinite Being. By revealing yourself, you will give others the courage to experience this truth."

The monastery meditation hall had always been somewhat dark, but now it gradually became brighter. Simultaneously, the room mysteriously seemed to grow into a huge, majestic, and beautifully appointed hall. The beat of Essa's heart quickened as he looked around the room. It was richly decorated with panels of gold silk, framing layers of purple veil from behind which light came. In places, beams of light shone like crystal-clear rods of jasper stone. And the foundations of the walls were garnished with all manner of precious stones that reflected the light in a thousand hues.

Bentell continued speaking, in a voice which was now exceedingly deep and strong: "There are seven awareness levels a person must go through. These levels can be called survival, reproduction, power, awareness, universal love, faith, and self-realization. All who take human form must eventually progress through them. Even you, Essa, needed to free yourself from these levels of karma. Only then are you able to get on with your real business."

Essa felt a tremendous surge in his spirit. His life energies burst forth. He rejoiced.

"Now is the time for your own great celebration feast," said Bentell. He led Essa along the hall, through the carved sandalwood columns and finally through a large doorway that he had never noticed previously.

Essa followed Bentell through the massive carved doors from which light streamed. Here was another tremendously large hall. This hall was shaped so that whichever way Essa looked, his attention was always directed toward the center. And in the center of the hall was a magnificent, round, hand-carved cinnabar table, supported on the four upturned trunks of carved elephants.

Sitting around the table were ten radiant men. Bentell beamed as he walked over to take his position at the table. He sat down with the others and looked at Essa. Essa didn't know what to do. His mouth opened, but he could not speak. He was stunned by the splendor of it all.

Bentell said, "Come closer and be with us." He beckoned for Essa to join him at the table. Essa was barely able to move his body, afraid that any movement on his part would dispel the vision, but with extreme effort he managed to walk to the table.

All eleven men arose, each holding up high a golden cup. They were real golden cups, but their curved and tapered shapes were strangely reminiscent of rams' horns.

Bentell spoke in an unusually loud and commanding voice, offering a blessing.

"Let us celebrate in the name of the One, Eternal Spirit. Think only of the One Spirit, One Power, One Substance. Lift up your cup, Essa, and rejoice. Let us drink of the Spirit together. Sing as we merge and become one.

"We were never separate from you. You were always perfect and whole. I wanted to tell you sooner, but you would not have heard. A shadow obstructed your vision so completely that you would not have seen. But you were not afraid to forego normal human comforts. You stood completely naked and alone and followed your destiny regardless of consequences.

"From the very beginning, you knew who you were. You had simply forgotten your true self. You are an illuminated soul, a master of wisdom, who has taken physical form to teach the truth and awaken mankind. You are the Alpha and Omega, the beginning and the end, the first and the last."

They all drank from their cups. Bentell continued: "Now we will break bread together and share in our boundless love. Eat and know that you may have life, and have it more abundantly. All that we have is yours. Eat and know that we were always with you. We will continue forever to be with you. We shall never leave or forsake you."

Essa was released from his last vestige of doubt and illusion. His former confusions now came clear to him. His heart became pure love and wisdom. He saw the infinite beauty of all existence. He was the beloved one. He was the anointed one.

Tears of joy flowed down Essa's cheeks. He was filled with emotion from this rare and great experience. Essa looked at the circle of men. There were now twelve of them. The circle was complete.

Bentell touched the center of Essa's forehead, saying "All that the Father is, you are. I call you my brother for we are one. Know that you and your Father are one. You were always one. You will always be one."

Every vestige of self-delusion disappeared. Essa felt his heart expand and encompass all of creation like a limitless and cloudless sky. His simple patched traveling robe changed into a light white garment of pure silk with a deep red and purple border. His soul was miraculously awakened. All his delusions were transformed into joy, and he felt the celebration of life within.

Peace and joy reigned among all twelve men who manifested the One. They were one consciousness, one life. In ecstatic celebration of divine life, they stood and raised their sacramental cups to shoulder height. In unison, they toasted the joy that spilled forth from their hearts.

They toasted the rebirth of Essa, now complete and whole. The toast was the chant used by the ancient Essene sect when new life was called forth.

"Fathered by the One.
The perfection of love, harmony and beauty.
The only being.
We are united with all the illuminated souls
who form the embodiment of the Master.
The Spirit of Guidance."

Essa was ordained. They put down their cups and joyfully gathered around Essa, embracing and giving thanks and praises for the beauty of the world and all creation.

Essa's heart was full of joy and he knew that his search had ended. He had traveled to the very core of his being. He had been empowered. He was complete. He and his Father were indeed One.

On that new morning, Bentell stood and quietly spoke: "Eventually each student must leave his teacher. Essa, that time is at hand. You are transformed, and now you must leave and return to your homeland. Go forth and fulfill your destiny."

EPILOG

Essa traveled west toward Galilee. He was enthralled by the beauty of the sunrise, the forests, the sparkling rivers, and all he saw. He took joy in his life. He was light and free. After seventeen years of absence, he returned to the land of his birth and rejoined his family.

On the third day back, he and his mother attended a wedding of his mother's relatives. It was a great celebration with much singing and dancing. There were more people than expected, so the host soon ran out of wine. Essa's mother asked him to provide more wine.

There were six stone jars, each filled with twenty or more gallons of water to be used for the ceremonial washing of hands. His thoughts stirred the water in the jars and he felt the power channel through him as the water became wine.

The steward, in disbelief, called the bridegroom and said to him, "Every man serves the good wine first; and when men have drunk freely, then the poor wine is brought out. But you have kept the good wine until now."

Essa walked away without answering. He knew it was time to begin his final ministry. My Father and I are one, he thought, and he smiled.